HEART OF THORNS

Thornwood Fae Book 1

NICOLETTE ANDREWS

Copyright © 2016 by Nicolette Andrews

Cover Art By Nadica Boshkovika

Cover Design By Covers By Combs

All rights reserved.

No part of this book may be reproduced in any form or by any electronic or mechanical means, including information storage and retrieval systems, without written permission from the author, except for the use of brief quotations in a book review.

To the authors who inspired me both living and dead. To Austen for awakening my love of regency romance and to Marrillier who introduced me to the world of the unseen fae.

ACKNOWLEDGMENTS

This book has been many years in the making. Now in its third iteration, I finally feel it has reached the vision I imagined when I first put pen to paper. There have been many people along the way who made this possible. First of all my beloved husband whose tireless hard work and support has allowed me the space to explore new worlds. My dear friends, Monika and Jessica, whose feedback helped shape this story and my editing team Kat and Charity who helped give this a final polish. Last but not least, the readers who've stuck with me all this time. Thank you all without you this book would not be possible.

PROLOGUE

Mum always said, "When the lanterns were lit, any respectable woman would be tucked in bed." But Evelyn refused to turn back, not now, not knowing how Miss Brown would gloat. She missed Mum and London, even the smell.

At least back home, there were gas lanterns to light your way if you were caught out after dark. Here in the country, nightfall cloaked her like a burial shroud, and the cavernous silence echoed with each footstep. A chill wind blew. Evelyn wrapped her shawl tighter around her shoulders. Each of her footfalls on the gravel crunched like the gnashing of teeth. She imagined a beast approaching her from behind, its hot breath on her neck. A dog howled, and she stumbled, teetering close to falling on her face.

A shadow darted across the road, and Evelyn's heart slammed against her rib cage. Perhaps it would be better to go back and face Miss Brown's mockery than risk being some monster's supper.

"Who's there?" A shiver ran up her spine.

Silence answered.

It was an animal. The howling had to have been an old farm dog. Evelyn looked back toward Thornwood Abbey. A few candles remained lit in the windows. Not everyone had gone to bed. Miss Brown must be waiting up to see her run back, scared. Miss Brown had warned her about the forest and how girls went missing from time to time. Evelyn had scoffed and dismissed it as simple, country folk superstition. As a girl, she used to pretend fairies would come to visit her and beg for sweets. But those were fairy tales and childish imagination.

The distant light of The Fairy Bride, the local pub, beckoned to her. A warm cider by the fire would take the bite out of her fear. And being among the working folk of the village would be a balm for the soul. An aching loneliness had settled on her since she'd arrived. She hoped the tenants and farmers were not like the posh servants back at Thornwood Abbey. They might welcome her into the community and soothe this longing for companionship. The other maids mocked her for her inexperience working in such a grand house. She'd have a drink and return before curfew. That would wipe the smug smile off Miss Brown's face.

A frigid wind ruffled her shawl and brushed chilly fingers along her nape. Footsteps thumped on the gravel behind her. She dared not check and instead burrowed into the thick fabric of her shawl and strode forward. Yellow light spilled from behind the opaque diamond-shaped glass of the Fairy Bride. The door swung open, and local patrons tumbled out, their laughter drifting on the air. Almost there.

Someone grabbed her shoulder.

Evelyn screamed and took a swing at her assailant, eyes

squeezed shut. They caught her wrist, and she pulled to escape, but they held on tight.

"Please let me go. I never did no harm to no one," she sobbed. Her chin wobbled.

His mocking laughter shocked her like a splash of cold water. Through tear-clustered lashes, she peered up at Mr. Thorn's smirking expression. His smile felt intimate, as if they were sharing a private joke, but she didn't know the punchline. Evelyn had never looked at him up close before or examined his uncanny features. Mr. Thorn's long hair bordered on obscene and framed his dark almond-shaped eyes that peered into her soul. In her twenty-one years, she had never seen a gentleman half as beautiful as Mr. Thorn, and he a gardener no less! It seemed ludicrous that someone as gorgeous as him spent his days toiling in the earth.

"Miss Smith, it's a bit late for you to be out and about," Mr. Thorn said.

"Mr. Thorn! You nearly scared the life outta me. I thought you were one of those terrible creatures Miss Brown warned me about." She'd worked herself into a frenzy over nothing. Fairies and monsters weren't real.

"There's no need to fear. It is only me," he said with a grin. "Since we have happened to meet, would you like to join me at The Fairy Bride for a drink?"

She pressed her hand to her lips to stifle the surprised "oh" that was threatening to spill from her lips. Mr. Thorn was a different sort of danger. Men who knew they were handsome wielded it like a sword. She knew better, of course. And had avoided him when he came around, or when the other maids tittered over him working in the gardens in nothing but his sweat-soaked undershirt...

To even consider a dalliance would be to spit in the face

3

of Mum's sacrifices. It had been Mum's dream that she work in the house of a highborn lord. She couldn't risk such a fortunate position by dallying with another member of the staff. Those types of things were what got a maid dismissed or worse with a baby in her belly and the man scarce.

On the other hand, it always took a while to make friends in a new place. The staff at Thornwood Abbey were a particularly closed-off lot. They were all born and raised in the village. When Mrs. Morgan selected Evelyn, an outsider for the coveted lady's maid position, it hadn't made matters any easier. She never thought she would be this lonely. Having someone to talk to would be nice. If they were in a public place, she would be safe from untoward advances.

"Miss Smith?" he prompted.

A flush burned her cheeks. "Yes, that would be lovely."

He offered her his bent arm, and she pressed the barest tips of her fingers to the cotton sleeve. Together they went into the pub, where he ordered her a drink. They sat at a table by the fire. The cider was spiced to perfection, and when Mr. Thorn's hand brushed against her, it set her entire body aflame. A village girl came by, batting long lashes at Mr. Thorn, but he dismissed her without taking his eyes off Evelyn. The night seemed to pass in a happy blur; one drink turned into several. And before she knew it, her head was pleasantly fuzzy.

"It's getting late. Shall I escort you home?" he asked.

"That would be lovely."

Mr. Thorn got up to settle the check. Whispers followed him. A few patrons remained. They crossed their arms and whispered to one another out of the corner of their mouths. The weight of their accusatory stares fell on her. Evelyn shifted in her seat. She didn't want to get a reputation among the village as being immoral. It seemed they were no different than Thornwood Abbey. How was she going to make a life here if the who neighbors were so hostile?

Perhaps it had been a mistake to come here with him. She'd been so swept up, she hadn't considered the consequences. If they left together, tongues would only wag further. Even if nothing happened, her reputation would be harmed. She slid out of the front door to wait for Mr. Thorn outside. She caught his eye on the way out, and he inclined his head as he smiled at her. Her heart filled with that warm glow all over again. Maybe she had misjudged him. Nothing about their interactions this evening had suggested any ill intent from him.

The cold outside did little to staunch her good cheer. Let the villagers think what they wanted. She'd done nothing wrong. Mr. Thorn had shown her kindness, unlike the rest of the stuck-up staff.

She rocked on the balls of her feet back and forth as she waited. Minutes passed, and Mr. Thorn did not join her. That village girl must have detained him. If she went back to check, it would only raise more questions. But she hated to walk home alone. Beyond the ring of yellow light from the Fairy Bride's window, darkness loomed. The creeping sensation of being watched had not gone away.

A song drifted on the night air. It wrapped around Evelyn like an embrace. It seemed to be coming from the woods across from the inn. The Fairy Bride sat along the main road that led to the village proper. As it did in much of Thornwood, the woods enclosed the building. Vines slid through cracks in stone walls, and roots disrupted paved roads.

The song pulled at Evelyn, calling her forward. *Come to us*, it seemed to be saying. *Dance, my child. Let your fears go.*

5

She inched toward the edge of the light where the path met the forest. The allure of the song was undeniable, but if she strayed too far, Mr. Thorn might think she'd gone ahead without him. Where was it coming from? And who was singing? She stepped into the shadows, hesitantly at first. As she drew closer, a sense of surety settled over her.

She stumbled over a rock and fell to her knees. Pain shot up her leg. The song stopped. Darkness enveloped her. Even the light of the Fairy Bride had disappeared. Had she wandered farther into the forest than she meant to?

It took her eyes a moment to adjust. A sliver of the moon gave little light. Tall trees loomed on all sides and blocked the road from view. A figure approached. The stars outlined his form in a thin string of light. He stood back and hid his face from view.

"Can you help me? I wandered from the road."

He did not speak and did not move to help her.

"I tripped over a rock. My mum used to say I'd trip over my own breath." She laughed as she stood. As she tried to regain her feet, he slammed her back down. Body pinned by the shoulders, she fought against him as he straddled her waist.

"What're you doin'?" She kicked her legs and wriggled her torso, trying to break free to no avail.

"Hush," Mr. Thorn said. His voice was husky, and his breath was warm against her face.

"What are—" he covered her mouth with his hand, stifling her words.

She tried to scream, thrash, make any noise. The pub was a few feet away. Someone would hear. Someone would come to help. Wouldn't they?

He tore her blouse with one hand. Her chest heaved with her shaking breaths.

"Please." Her pleas were muffled by his hand as hot tears rolled down her cheeks.

A cold knife brushed her skin as he cut through her gown and petticoat. Her flesh pimpled in the evening's chill.

"Don't worry, my pet. I don't want your body. I'm only after your heart," he whispered into her ear as he thrust the knife hilt-deep into her chest.

1

The woman in white crept toward Catherine. Her eyes, like bottomless pits, bored into her.

Catherine froze on the threshold of the morning room. The woman in white inched closer even as a servant walked through her as if she were made of mist.

Catherine closed her eyes and counted to ten as Dr. Armstrong had taught her. She wasn't real. She wasn't there.

She opened them, and the woman in white's gaunt face filled her vision. A red stain spread out from the empty chasm where her heart had been cut out. Catherine jerked her head backward and pressed her hand to her mouth to suppress her scream. The servants, who were busy placing dishes on the long table covered in crisp white linen, didn't notice Catherine. She couldn't catch her breath; her heart pounded. Not today, not on the first morning of her new life. Lord Thornton would arrive at any moment and find her staring at nothing. He would ask unwanted questions, questions she'd been trying to avoid since they met.

Counting always worked before, but if she couldn't

shake the vision, perhaps she could just ignore her. Closing her eyes, Catherine marched forward, stiff-legged, over to the banquet table. When she opened her eyes, the ghost was gone, and rows of gleaming silver cloches in a row awaited her. First breakfast. Though she had no stomach for it, she would go through the motions at least. Hands trembling, she reached for the cloche that covered the dish in front of her. An icy hand curled on her shoulder. Catherine yelped and threw her hands up, dropping it. It struck another platter and made a loud bang as it crashed onto the floor.

All eyes turned to Catherine, including the dead stare of the ghost whose glacial grip had not slackened on her shoulder. A shiver ran through her.

The ghost touched her.

They never touched her.

A chill sliced her down to the marrow.

"Lady Thornton, please let us serve you," Mr. Hobbs, the butler, said as he picked up the cloche.

She stepped out of the way and out of the grip of the ghost. Mr. Hobbs hardly came up to Catherine's chin, and over the top of his head, the woman in white watched her with hooded black eyes. Not real. Not real. She chanted it in her head over and over like a talisman.

Being in a strange place, the uncertainty of her position was taking a toll upon her mental health. She was having a fit, nothing more. Catherine stared at the bald spot on the top of Mr. Hobbs' head as he nodded to the footmen who uncovered steaming mounds of sausage, toast, and eggs. The scent of cooked meat and eggs turned her stomach. Mr. Hobbs ladled hefty portions onto her plate, more than she could ever possibly eat. At Elk Grove, breakfast consisted of cold gruel in a chipped bowl. The staff didn't let them have hot meals in case a resident burned themselves.

The woman in white hovered at the fringes of her vision and swatted at Catherine's arm; the ghostly hand passed through her and raised her gooseflesh. Catherine yanked her arm back and elbowed Mr. Hobbs.

He turned to her with a pinched expression. "Lady Thornton?"

"That's plenty," she mumbled.

"As you wish, my lady," he said with narrowed eyes.

A footman pulled out a chair at the table beneath a window. Outside, the sky was a muted gray, and the garden beyond was obscured by fog. Mr. Hobbs carried her plate for her, and Catherine took a seat. She kept her head down to avoid the woman in white who continued to hover around her. The visions never lingered. They were never this insistent. What had changed? Was she getting worse? Hands in her lap, Catherine tugged at the hem of her sleeve hard enough to rip. She'd come this far; she wouldn't go back. Not to Elk Grove, not to the room. If she were to be Lady Thornton, she had to act like it.

Catherine picked up her fork off the table and clenched it so hard the metal bit into her hand. She stabbed her soft-boiled egg, and the yellow yolk bled across the blue pattern of the china. The woman in white stood in the center of the table, the white table cloth severing her torso as she leaned in, so they were nose to nose.

"He is coming for you next. Leave while you can," the woman in white said.

Catherine set her fork back down and took a long shuddering breath, and closed her eyes. *Get through breakfast. Greet her husband. Be the perfect wife.* The footman and Mr. Hobbs hovered at the edge of the room, staring blank-eyed forward. How could anyone eat like this?

The large, oaken doors to the morning room swung open with a groan. Catherine's head shot up. Blessedly the ghost was gone at last. Mrs. Morgan, the housekeeper, strode into the room, one hand clutching the ring of keys at her hip. Catherine sat up straighter in her chair. Mrs. Morgan's high-collared black gown and her severe expression reminded her of a cruel nurse back at Elk Grove who struck patients who behaved badly.

"Lady Thornton, good morning. I hope everything is to your liking," Mrs. Morgan said briskly.

"It is, thank you," Catherine said and bit her bottom lip.

"Do you have anything I can help you with?"

Catherine wrung her hands together. "When will Lord Thornton be joining me?"

"His lordship takes breakfast in his study."

"Oh."

"The former Lady Thornton took her breakfast in bed," Mrs. Morgan said with a sniff.

Catherine blushed. She had assumed even someone as high born as Lord Thornton would share his morning meal with his family. When she'd been a girl, she had loved eating with Mama and Papa and enjoyed talking about their plans for the day. But it seemed she had a lot to learn about how to be a lady, if she wanted to keep her husband happy.

"Then tomorrow, I suppose I shall as well."

"As you wish, my lady," Mrs. Morgan said, her lips curling. "His lordship sent me to tell you that he 'apologizes for not joining you on your first day at Thornwood Abbey but he hopes you be at your leisure and he will see you tonight for the dinner party.'"

The dinner party. She'd almost forgotten. Lord Thornton insisted on having some friends from the neighborhood over to make introductions. After everything he'd done for her and her family, how could she refuse him anything? Even if crowds made her uncomfortable, she must endure it. When she was a girl, the symptoms were at their worst when Mama hosted parties. Tonight she would need to take extra care as to not make a scene. The last thing she wanted was for Lord Thornton to discover her madness. She needed to escape outdoors to feel the wind on her face, bury her hands in earth. At Elk Grove, working in the garden had always calmed her. Her surroundings might have changed, but nature remained the same. Catherine stood, pushing off from the table. Her chair screeched as it scraped across the parquet floor.

"I look forward to it," she lied. "If it's not any trouble, could I go walk about the garden?"

"As you wish, my lady. I'll call Miss Larson to bring your coat." Mrs. Morgan headed for the door.

Catherine heaved a sigh of relief.

Mrs. Morgan stopped on the threshold and turned to Catherine, her expression serious. "Be sure to stay away from the woods by the south end. It is wild, and people have been known to lose their way among the trees."

The hairs on the back of Catherine's neck stood on end. On their way to Thornwood, they'd ridden through dense forest. The entire village seemed to be shrouded in mist and trees. It was sensible advice for someone new here but the creeping feeling of dread coiled around her. She looked over her shoulder to make sure the woman in white wasn't hovering around her once more.

Miss Larson brought Catherine a light blue coat, a straw

bonnet with white trim, and brown lace-up boots. Dressed for the outdoors, Catherine stepped out into the chilly morning air. Fog shrouded the landscape. A fountain burbled at the center of the circular drive, which led up to black iron gates and the village beyond. Dense forest peaked through the mist. It encircled Thornwood Abbey on all sides. Mrs. Morgan's warning rang in her ears. If she stuck to the garden paths, she would be fine. A dirt path wrapped around the back of Thornwood Abbey, and she headed in that direction.

Dew clung to the lawn and soaked the hem of her skirt as she brushed against it. The air here in the country felt crisp and clean. Gravel crunched pleasantly beneath her boots. Flashes of green shrubbery peeked between veils of gray fog. Ash and oak trees lined the path, which led to a white Grecian style gazebo with marble benches to sit upon. Catherine brushed her hands against the cool stone. It kept winding upward and through a hedge maze. The acres that surrounded Thornwood Abbey were expansive, and she could see herself exploring for months or years and still not uncovering all of its secrets.

She passed by the hedge maze, promising herself to visit another day, and headed to a barren row of the orchard at the far end of a grassy field. In her favorite book, Lady of the Moors, Tristan, the novel's hero, professed his love to Angelique in an orchard. Catherine strolled beneath the skeletal branches and grasped one with a single bud waiting to bloom. This small vessel brimmed with potential life, a flower, and later fruit. Right now, the garden slumbered, but this bud was a promise of spring. It had always been her favorite time of the year, nudging the plants to awaken, and seeing their petals and leaves unfurl to bask in the sunlight after the cold winter.

Catherine's thoughts swirled with plans for plantings. Would it be too bold to ask Lord Thornton for a little patch of earth to call her own? There was so much here, and many parts had grown wild. Just in case, she hunted about for the perfect location, one which would get the right amount of sunlight and shade but also wouldn't attract attention. What she liked most about gardening was the silence and solitude of it where she could be alone without fear of others.

As she wandered, Catherine came upon a patch of tangled vines a few meters from the path. The star-shaped leaves with dark green tips and pale green centers were like nothing she'd seen before. She went to investigate.

A breeze prickled the hairs on the back of her neck. Catherine looked up as the fog shifted, exposing a copse of tangled dark trees. Two dark, knotty oaks grew side by side, and their boughs entwined together as if they'd grown that way. Their branches fused together, and it was impossible to see where one began, and the other ended. The strange vine tangled between them. On closer inspection, she could see pinky-sized black thorns. She'd never seen anything quite like it.

A faint song drifted on the wind. Catherine strained her ears to hear it. It seemed to be coming from behind this thorny oak. She inched closer, careful not to scratch herself on the thorns. The unearthly song became clearer though the words were spoken in a language she did not know. The singer sounded as if they could be a man or a woman. Though she didn't know the words, it beckoned to her. They wanted her to step through the doorway. Her eyes darted over the trees and vines. If she squinted, it nearly looked like a pair of doors. What a strange tree. Catherine extended a hand toward the twin oaks, her finger hovering over the point of a thorn.

"Be careful," an amused male voice said.

Catherine jolted backward and threw her hands up.

"I didn't mean—" Catherine said.

A handsome man with long, dark hair and a tall, lean build stood a foot from her. His white teeth flashed as he smiled at her. His beauty unnerved her. Once, when she was very young, she thought a beautiful glowing man with pointed ears had appeared from among the trees in a park in London. When she had told Mama about him, she had told her to not make up stories. That man wasn't real, though. Like the ghosts and other things she saw, they were just figments of an insane mind. Catherine closed her eyes and counted to ten.

He chuckled. "Are you hoping I will go away if you close your eyes? It doesn't work that way."

She opened her eyes. He hadn't disappeared. Perhaps she had made a mistake? He wasn't translucent as a ghost, nor did he have pointed ears like the man in the park. Catherine pressed her hand to her mouth. What had she done? She should say something, or he might rightfully think her insane.

"Pardon me, I thought I was alone." Catherine bowed her head and addressed the ground.

"Not many people wander this far from Thornwood or this close to the Thorn Dweller's woods." He took a step closer to her. His gaze was fixed upon her, and it made her heart race. His eyes were a vibrant green.

"Thorn Dweller's woods?" She swallowed past a lump in her throat as she gestured to the pair of oaks.

"Did no one warn you about these woods? These woods

are home to the Thorn Dwellers. Those that hear their song are lured into their world and never come out again." Another step. Her heart must have been pounding hard enough for him to hear it now. Was that why Mrs. Morgan had warned her to stay away? But what were the Thorn Dwellers? It sounded like a fearsome creature, but there was no such thing.

"They did. I apologize. I'll be going then. It was a pleasure, Mr...?"

"My apologies, my lady. My name is Ray. Ray Thorn." He smirked.

The hairs on her arms stood on end. The unearthly song had lured her here, and the tales of creatures in the woods made her uneasy. It was all likely superstitious nonsense, but she would not linger a moment longer. With a quick bow of her head, Catherine ran for Thornwood Abbey and not once looked back, fearing if she did both he and the forest would be gone.

2

Catherine picked at the fabric of her silken gloves as voices drifted up from the parlor. The guests had already arrived. She hooked a finger under the string of pearls she wore. They'd been a gift from Lord Thornton. For most of her life at Elk Grove, she'd lived in rough spun cotton dresses. Patients weren't permitted anything finer than that.

Along with the pearls, he'd given her an emerald green dress made of silk and lace. It was covered in intricate beading, and layers of fabric, and the weight of it felt as if it might crush her. The hallway that led from her room ended upon a landing overlooking the foray. To each side of her were curved staircases that led down onto the main floor. After her lady's maid, Miss Larson, had dressed her in Lord Thornton's gifts, she was told to wait here to make their grand entrance.

While she waited on Lord Thornton, the sun set. The broad windows across from the landing let in the pink and purple light of another dying day. Servants came around and lit the chandelier that hung above the foyer.

Night swallowed the interior of Thornwood Abbey as the sun sank below the tree line. To each side of her, the wings of the manor were veiled in darkness. A pale face hovered at the end of the hallway.

Catherine looked down at her feet as she rubbed her arm where her skin pebbled. Footsteps approached. She swallowed past the lump in her throat and took a second look. A maid lit the candle sconces along the walls, and flickering light danced on the dark-wood panels. Her face had been illuminated by the candle. Catherine had mistaken her for a ghost.

Catherine exhaled. Parties already made her nervous. She didn't need the added complication of another fit. She didn't want to give a bad impression to Lord Thornton's family. Everything had to be perfect.

A pale hand with blackened nails wrapped around the banister beside her. The woman in white was back. Catherine squeezed her eyes shut. There was nothing there. It wasn't real. Not tonight. Please spare her just this evening. She counted down from ten. Apart from the distant chatter of their guests, the manor creaked, and the wind blew outside the windows like a sad lament or a painful moan. It was, in a way, a strange comfort. Each night at Elk Grove, she'd fallen asleep to the cries of the other residents.

A hand clasped upon her shoulder. They were going to take her to the room! Catherine lurched back, and her rear brushed against the banister, and she threw her hands out to steady herself. Lord Thornton seized her arm. Catherine tensed her shoulders, screwed her eyes shut, and pressed her lips together to stifle a whimper of fear.

"Catherine, I beg your pardon. I didn't mean to startle you," Lord Thornton said.

She peeked her eye open and took in Lord Thornton's face. He stood close enough that she could see the faintest freckling on his cheekbones. Lord Thornton didn't try to drag her to the room, nor reprimand her. His mouth turned down at the corners. When he grabbed her arm, she had acted on impulse. This wasn't Elk Grove, and Lord Thornton was not one of the nurses or Dr. Armstrong. She was safe here.

"Lord Thornton, forgive me," she said, a little breathless as her cheeks burned.

"We're married now. You should call me Edward, and I will call you Catherine. Lord and Lady Thornton sounds much too formal, don't you think?" He put his finger under her chin, lifting her gaze to his.

"If it would please you... Edward," she mumbled as she averted her gaze.

It felt wrong to address him in such a way. She was beneath him. He claimed he loved her, but she couldn't say with confidence she returned that feeling. She hadn't married for love but out of desperation. Either she marry him, or return to the asylum. Wearing this fine gown and gloves, having a servant dress her and do her hair. It felt unnatural. As did being called "my lady". She felt as if she had donned a costume and was to take part in a play. But she didn't know the lines.

Mrs. Morgan ascended the stairs toward them. Lord Thornton took a step back from her, and Catherine let out a breath.

"My lord, the guests are waiting," Mrs. Morgan said.

"Then we shouldn't keep them waiting for another moment. Shall we?" Edward smiled and offered his bent arm.

Edward was like the hero of a novel, but she wasn't a heroine. Her fingertips grazed the crook of his arm. If she didn't want to go back to Elk Grove, then she had to play her part, even if she had to make it up as she went along. They descended the stairs together and paused before the bright parlor. All the sconces had been lit, and the fire crackled. Two women, one with brown wavy hair and one with ebony hair streaked with gray, sat side by side on a sofa, chatting. Opposite them, a dark-haired gentleman read the evening paper. Catherine's heart thundered in her chest.

"Lady and Lord Thornton," Mr. Hobbs announced.

The ladies looked up while the gentleman continued reading.

She felt the weight of their stares as the brunette looked her up and down and the older dark-haired woman beamed at her.

"At last, the mystery is solved. We can now feast our eyes upon the enigmatic Lady Thornton!" The brunette woman flounced over to them. Her glistening chestnut ringlets bounced, and the pearls at her throat flashed in the candlelight.

"Lydia—" Edward said in a warning tone.

"I told Mr. Oakheart that it must be a ruse. What brother would marry without so much as a post to inform his sister or invite her to the ceremony? How could you be so cold-hearted, Edward?" She playfully struck at his shoulder.

This must be the sister Edward had mentioned. He had been in such a rush to get married, Catherine hadn't questioned how it would affect his family. Catherine shuffled her feet as she pulled her hand out of the crook of Edward's arm.

"You wouldn't have left the country for the ceremony even if he had," said the older woman with dark hair. She was shorter than Lydia, but her smile brightened her heart-shaped face.

"At least he wrote and gave you the news beforehand. Can you imagine finding out your brother is getting married from your aunt!" Lydia crossed her arms over her chest as she jutted out her bottom lip.

"Shush. Lady Thornton is going to think we're uncivilized," said Lydia's aunt. "Please, forgive my niece; she does not always think before she speaks. I am Isobel Rosewood, Edward's aunt, and this is Lydia Oakheart, his elder sister."

"Elder! You make it sound as if I am ancient," Lydia protested.

"Forgive my sister's rudeness. She is rather excitable." Edward reached for Catherine's hand and threaded their fingers together.

Lydia arched a brow as he did so. Then with a smile, she linked arms with Catherine. "Come sit; I've been dying to meet you."

Lydia practically dragged Catherine across the room and sat her down on the sofa across from the gentleman who had not once looked up from his paper.

"That is my dear husband, Mr. Oakheart. Say hello, dear." Lydia flapped a hand in his direction.

He rustled his paper. "Hello."

"I must know everything about Edward and your torrid love affair. Where did you meet? What did you wear at the wedding? Who are your parents? Do you know the Johnsons? They're dear friends of ours who moved to London. Or what about the Bells? Mr. Oakheart went to Cambridge with Mr. Bell, and I met his lovely wife last we visited."

Catherine opened and closed her mouth to reply but couldn't answer a question before another one was being asked. Edward stood at the arm of Mrs. Rosewood's chair, shaking his head.

"Lydia, give the girl a moment to breathe," Mrs. Rosewood chided.

"Can you blame me for being curious? Just last month, all Edward could talk about was Miss Ashton—"

"Shall we head to dinner then?" Edward clapped his hands together.

"That's enough." Mr. Oakheart set his paper down at last.

Lydia glared at Mr. Oakheart, and they shared a silent exchange. Edward strode over to the pull chain on the wall. A hidden bell then rang to summon a servant. No one looked at Catherine, to her relief. It might be too much to hope she would get through the rest of the dinner unnoticed. She shifted uncomfortably in her seat, smoothing out wrinkles in her gown. It was just one dinner, smile, play her part. Nothing more.

The fireplace crackled and popped. Who was Miss Ashton? A former lover, perhaps? Had Edward been rejected and sought to seek comfort in the arms of another? That's how it happened in novels. It would explain why he had been so insistent on marrying quickly. Catherine squirmed in her seat as she tugged at the fingers of her glove.

Mr. Hobbs arrived and saved them all from the awkward silence. Edward collected her from the sofa, and together they led the way into the dining room. Dark wood panels lined the room. The dining table was draped in ivory linen. Bouquets of pink peonies, purple roses, and buttery daffodils were artfully arranged in crystal vases. Five footmen in black coats and pristine white gloves drew out their chairs for them as they entered. Edward sat at the head of the table and Catherine to his right. Lydia and her husband took the seats across from her, and Mrs. Rosewood to her right.

The savory scent of a creamy mushroom and herb soup proceeded the footmen who served it to the guests starting with Edward.

A footman with ginger hair ladled a thick spoonful into her bowl. Catherine stared at her steaming bowl of soup. Bits of green herbs floated amongst chunks of mushroom. On either side of her bowl were a multitude of gleaming forks and spoons glittering in the candlelight. Which utensil did she use? Dining at Elk Grove had been mostly with tarnished spoons and bowls of gruel. When she'd returned home, Mama had tried to teach her etiquette, but everything she had taught her flew out of her mind. She bunched her hands in her lap and twisted the fabric of her skirt in a fist.

Mrs. Oakheart watched her with a small curl of her lips. They'd just met, and it felt as if she already saw through Catherine's facade. An insane woman and daughter of an impoverished gentleman wasn't worthy of one of the gentry. Perhaps Mrs. Oakheart knew that Papa had been spared of debtor's prison thanks to Edward's intervention.

"Start from the outside and work your way in from that spoon," Mrs. Rosewood leaned in to whisper in Catherine's ear.

Catherine smiled at her and mouthed a thank you. The knots in her stomach untangled. Perhaps she could take a few bites of food. She took a few spoonfuls of her soup. The cream was luxurious, and the combination of rosemary and what she thought was thyme made for a complex flavor palate. The warmth and richness of the dish warmed her.

They finished the soup course without further incident.

While servants were bringing in the second course, the footmen brought around a bowl of water for Catherine and the other guests to dip their fingers in. She'd never been to a dinner party quite like this, and the rituals were strange, but any time she got lost, Mrs. Rosewood gave her discreet guidance. A footman with dark hair and a large nose brought in the main course: a whole roasted goose surrounded by carrots and roasted potatoes. Everyone complimented the bird as Mr. Hobbs carved the breast and put it on plates.

"Edward, don't keep us in suspense any longer. How did you and Lady Thornton meet?" Lydia cast a sly look at Edward as she cut into her dinner.

Lord Thornton glared back at her. They shared a silent exchange as if they were speaking some wordless language only they knew.

"We met by chance at a dinner party, at a friend of Aunt Isobel's, Mrs. Wells. I was rather taken with Catherine upon her first meeting, and then I happened to run into her again the next day while I was out for my daily walk."

"Quite the chance meeting, indeed." Mrs. Oakheart glanced over toward Catherine with a raised brow.

Catherine lowered her gaze to her dinner plate and pushed around the roasted potato and carrot. How could she make Lydia like her? She had her pegged as a social ladder climber, and she wasn't entirely wrong.

"We are very fortunate Edward met someone who makes him happy. Don't you think this is cause for celebration?" Mrs. Rosewood asked.

Lydia pressed her lips together and sniffed.

Catherine's face and neck burned. If she had the choice, she would run away or let the floor swallow her up.

Mr. Oakheart cleared his throat. Catherine had almost

forgotten he was there. He'd said hardly a word all evening. "Mrs. Rosewood is right; we are here to celebrate the happy couple. Let's have us a toast then." Mr. Oakheart raised a glass.

"A splendid idea, to the happy couple!" Mrs. Rosewood raised her glass as well.

Catherine curled her fingers around her own glass. Lydia pursed her lips and grasped her goblet as they toasted.

Catherine swallowed her bittersweet wine in one gulp. It lodged in her throat as she set her glass down heavily. She clutched the stem of her glass harder to stop fidgeting.

"Speaking of celebrations. It's been too long since we've had a ball at Thornwood Abbey. What if we have one to celebrate Lady Thornton's arrival?" Edward said.

Lydia perked up, her eyes bright. "That is a splendid idea! We could invite the entire neighborhood. It's been ages since we had a ball!" She clapped her hands together.

Any ill feelings were seemingly forgotten as Lydia chattered about plans for the ball, fondly recalling her own debut ball. No one noticed Catherine as she pushed her food around her plate. A crawling feel of anxiety swept over her. The dinner party had been hard enough to manage; a ball might be ten times worse. But she pressed her lips together, not willing to voice dissent when the decision had been made already without her input.

After dinner, the ladies went to the salon, while Edward and Mr. Oakheart hung back in the dining room to smoke cigars. When Mama hosted parties, Papa and the other men would smoke cigars and talk business. Catherine assumed Edward would do much the same, though she felt vulnerable being left alone with his aunt and sister and without him there to shield her.

Lydia had taken a seat by the fire, and the way she watched Catherine as she entered the room was reminiscent of a hawk prepared to swoop down onto its prey. Catherine steeled herself, ready for a confrontation, or at least veiled accusations as to Catherine's character. She could do this, just get through the evening. All that mattered was Edward; he held the keys to her fate. Though she would have liked for his sister to like her.

"Lady Thornton, would you be so kind as to walk about the room with me? It helps my digestion," Mrs. Rosewood asked.

The request could not have been better timed. She linked arms with her, and they strolled around the room while Lydia watched them with a narrowed gaze. Twice tonight, Mrs. Rosewood had come to her rescue.

"Don't mind Lydia too much. She's not accustomed to not getting what she wants. And she and Miss Ashton have been plotting the two of them becoming sisters since they were girls."

"I didn't want to cause any trouble..." Catherine whispered.

Mrs. Rosewood pulled her chin up. "There is nothing to apologize for. You are the Lady Thornton and the woman our Edward chose. You should be proud of that. Lydia will come around in time, don't worry."

Coming here, Catherine had been so uncertain, so afraid. And while she still had her doubts, there was something about Lady Rosewood's words that gave her comfort. Perhaps here in Thornwood Abbey, she could find a sense of normalcy and a life she thought only existed in stories. They made another pass around the room, and Catherine was feeling better. Then she lifted her head. The woman in white watched her from the corner. The red stain on her gown stark and the hole in her chest made a grotesque unblinking eye that stared into Catherine's soul. She lifted a pale hand and pointed it at Catherine.

"You're next."

3

Heavy footsteps roused Ray from his dozing. Not that he needed sleep, but there wasn't much else to do at Thornwood. His visitor huffed and grumbled under his breath. Ray kept his eyes closed. The orchard had been the perfect nap spot. On the cusp between winter and spring, the humans rarely strolled here, and until the fall harvest, the gardeners rarely came this way either apart from the winter pruning. Now he would need to find a new hiding spot. How bothersome.

"Enjoying a little nap, I see?" Mr. Rockwell growled.

Or was it Mr. Gardner? No, wait. Mr. Berry? No, no. Mr. Berry had been the head gardener decades ago. After a century trapped in Thornwood, all the head gardeners started to blend together. He cracked open an eye. Beady black eyes shaded by a hooded brow glared down at Ray. This one was Mr. Rockwell. He remembered now because the man had a barrel chest and tree trunk-sized arms like a rock troll. The intelligence of one too.

"Why, Mr. Rockwell, to what do I owe the pleasure?" Ray said through a yawn as he stretched.

"I instructed you to rake the mulch in the orchard, and here I find you," Mr. Rockwell said. His teeth creaked as he grit them.

"You're right; I should have hidden better," Ray agreed. Now he remembered what had inspired his decision to nap here. A miscalculation, to be certain.

"Don't get cheeky with me, I ought to knock that smug head of yours off." Mr. Rockwell clenched a fist as a vein pulsed in his neck. He might actually do it this time. The charm Ray had slipped him must be wearing off. As soon as he wandered out of sight, Mr. Rockwell should have forgotten any instruction he'd given Ray.

Ray glanced up at the gray clouds gathering in the sky. How many days until the full moon? He couldn't make another charm until then. It would be amusing if he threw a punch, though it would complicate things a bit. Then again, with how dreadfully boring Thornwood Abbey had been, a complication might liven up his day.

"Are you ignoring me?" Mr. Rockwell barked.

"No, I'm debating the merits of letting you take a swing at me."

"Why you!" He lumbered closer and swung a meaty fist at Ray's head, which he dodged.

Ray spun around, hands behind his back. Mr. Rockwell had a bit of troll blood. Maybe giant blood that had been generations diluted. Humans never got this big and angry without a bit of that in them.

"I don't want to hurt you," Ray said calmly.

Mr. Rockwell's face turned violet as he roared and rushed toward Ray. Ray sidestepped him again. Mr. Rockwell had swung first. The council couldn't scold him if he were just defending himself, but he didn't want to have to create a new identity to stay close to the gateway if Mr. Rockwell tried to fire him. He'd only just taken on this identity.

"You disrespectful little—" Mr. Rockwell trailed off as his face paled, eyes wide.

Ray turned to see a young human brunette, head lowered, her shoulders pulled up to her ears like a dog who had been struck one too many times. A perfect distraction to escape this confrontation. Now to catch Mr. Rockwell's eye and use his glamour to distract him. It was a short-term solution, but if he could avoid him until the full moon, he could avoid the mess of creating a new persona.

"Lady Thornton!" Mr. Rockwell removed his hat, exposing his thinning black hair. "Forgive my rudeness. I didn't see you there."

"Oh, I apologize. If you are busy, I can come back another time." She started to shuffle backward. Her eyes flickered in Ray's direction and then back to the ground.

They met again. Lady Thornton, who had somehow stumbled upon the gateway. She would need to be glamoured to erase her memories of the gateway. But to do so, she would first need to look him in the eye. And she was doing her best to not do just that.

"I've been expecting you, Lady Thornton." Ray clapped his hands together.

Her head jerked up, and she stared at him wide-eyed, her gaze darting from him to Mr. Rockwell. "You were?"

"Yes. Lord Thornton instructed me that I should take all my orders regarding the garden from you," Ray smiled, weaving in a bit of his glamour into the words.

"He did? But I didn't tell him I planned..." Her fingers

twitched at her side as her gaze darted around the misty lawns and toward the barren fruit trees. It was as if she expected something to leap out at her at any moment.

She shouldn't be asking questions; she should have agreed blindly. Was his glamour weakening as well?

"Why would Lord Thornton come to you?" Mr. Rockwell balked.

Ray pivoted to face him and caught Mr. Rockwell's beady black gaze. "Don't you remember you were there? You gave instructions that I would be at Lady Thornton's mercy." Ray glamoured his words, pouring in more magic than usual.

Mr. Rockwell's eyes glazed over as his heavy brow furrowed, and his dark caterpillar eyebrows pulled together. "Yea. That's right..." He scratched his balding head. "I'll leave you to it then." He then wandered away, wobbling like a drunkard.

Perhaps he'd used a bit too much magic. But if his glamour wasn't weakened, why was Lady Thornton immune? Curious. It would seem he'd found something to ease his boredom after all.

"Shall we start in the vegetable gardens?" He spread out his arm, gesturing toward the dirt path that led to it.

"Yes!" she said as she jolted upright. She scurried forward, glancing backward at him every few steps. What was she afraid of from him, exactly?

All her predecessors had cared about were vegetables and pretty flowers all in a row. Food for their larders and decorations for their tables. Humans were simple and predictable.

At a glance, Lady Thornton had seemed no different than any of the Lady Thorntons before her. He had assumed she found the gateway by mistake. Humans stumbled upon the gateway every now and again. Sometimes when the veil was thin, they fell through into Faery. When they managed to escape, they spread tales of magic portals and strange creatures dancing by moonlight. Humans, being distrustful, never believed and called such accounts fairy tales.

He'd thought Lady Thornton was another one of those hapless humans. But perhaps he'd been too quick to judge. She kept her head down as she walked, avoiding his gaze. Avoiding another attempt at glamouring her?

A stone wall about hip height surrounded the vegetable garden. Ray rushed ahead to open the creaking gate for her. She bobbed her head in thanks as she stepped inside, her hands twisted in front of her.

The sticky, sweet scent of honey cakes wafted from the kitchen a mere yard away. Ray's stomach growled. Normally he would have popped in to nick a few cakes. But he supposed as guardian of the gateway, he should at least make an attempt at investigating Lady Thornton.

"Any vegetable or herbs you'd like to have us grow, my lady?" Ray asked, gesturing toward the rows of greens.

She cast a quick glance over them and shook her head.

The vegetable garden had been merely a pretense to study her further, but he had assumed she would say more than a few words at a time. She glanced furtively at him from the corner of her eye. Was it all an act? If she were pretending, maybe she'd come looking for him to get the measure of him as well? A part of him delighted in the prospect. It had been a while since a human had intrigued him so. He hoped she didn't disappoint like so many others of her kind.

"Shall we move on with our tour then?" he asked.

She bit her lip. "Yes, thank you."

She lagged behind him as he led her back through the orchard and down and around toward the flower beds that lined the hedge maze. One of the former Lady Thorntons, he couldn't remember which, had insisted on creating the unnatural monstrosity. A living plant shouldn't be square and orderly, nor should blooms be decapitated to decorate a human's dinner table. But humans had many strange quirks he didn't understand despite all the time he lived among them.

"Oh," Lady Thornton gasped.

"My lady, did you fall?" Ray turned back to her.

She'd fallen to the ground, one hand braced in the grass damp with dew. Ray approached her cautiously. It might be a trick. Her tapered fingers stroked the cluster of thin leaves of a common plant the gardeners yanked out whenever they saw it. In this neglected corner of the garden, it had flourished, and an umbel of tight white buds swayed atop its leggy stem. It would bloom in a few days, a bouquet of tiny blossoms. Shame, the humans would tear it out if they found it.

"Cow parsley used to grow wild around Elk Grove," she practically cooed at the sprout like someone would a dog.

He'd never seen a human care so much for a plant, let alone one that most humans considered useless. The flowers were too small, not flashy enough to present, and the plant itself provided no nourishment. He'd only seen forest nymphs treat their saplings this tenderly.

That was it! She must be part nymph or some other sort from the low courts who'd had a dalliance with a human. It was common enough, especially with Thornwood being so close to a gateway.

She stood. A light dusting of earth clung to her skirt, which she didn't brush away. "If it's alright, I'd like to work here. I think it needs a tender touch." She turned an adoring gaze back on the patch of tangled grasses.

"This is a rather far away spot. There are nicer flower beds closer to the house where you can view them from your window," he said. If she were lingering around here, it meant going even further afield to hide out from Mr. Rockwell and his ceaseless demands for him to do his work. After a century of not doing his job as a gardener, he had no intention of starting now.

She flushed. "Well, you might find this silly, but I want to help the dandelions and nettle as well. The bees and wild animals rather like them, and it seems that the gardeners pull them out in those other flower beds. I know most people don't like looking at them, but they're living plants too..." She trailed off.

Very peculiar indeed. And rather charming, he had to admit. It had been quite a while since he'd taken a lover. Lady Thornton was pleasing to the eye, by human standards. And considering the puzzle she presented, this Lady Thornton might be worth getting to know.

Clouds obscured the sun, and Ray looked up. The sky had been rather gray, but this was nearly black. Would it rain?

"You must get away from him." A voice slithered into his ear. Ray turned, trying to find the source. A thick fog rolled in and surrounded them both, blocking the rest of the garden from view and carrying with it the stench of decay and a creeping chill.

Lady Thornton trembled as white puffs of breath escaped her lips.

A weak shadow moved around the perimeter. When Ray reached for it, he grasped only a handful of mist. Lady Thornton gasped, and he turned to see a female ghost. Black stained her hands and crept up to her elbows. She'd lingered too long past her death, and her soul had begun to decay. She leaned into Lady Thornton, who screwed her eyes shut. She knew enough to ignore it; that was good. Acknowledging them only made them stronger.

He hummed a few bars of an old song he had learned from the villagers centuries ago. "Lady Thornton, it does seem a fog is rolling in. Should I escort you back to the manor?"

"Uh, yess—" She cracked one eye open, saw the ghost, and squeezed them shut again. It was a rather persistent ghost; they usually moved on quickly, looking for easy prey to suck the energy from.

"You cannot go anywhere with him. He'll cut out your heart as he did me!" The ghost screeched and grasped for Lady Thornton's shoulders, but her hands passed through her.

Did the ghost mean him? He'd had many a slanderous thing said about him, and much of it was true. This was the first time he'd been accused of murder. Death had a way of confusing the deceased. Those that lingered grew more confused and more hostile. The best thing to do was for them both to ignore her. He grasped Lady Thornton by the elbow in an attempt to lead her away, but she wrenched her arm from him as she backed away, staring at him wide-eyed.

She believed this addled ghost? Well, now, he was offended. They'd only just met, and she already assumed the worst of him.

"Don't touch her!" The ghost hissed and held out her arms as she faced him, revealing her carved up torso. Her killer had cut out her heart. What cruel monster had done this to her? There were those among the fae who delighted in such cruelty. It might explain the ghost's confusion.

"I think it is time you've moved on. If you don't, then you'll only degrade further and lose all memory of who you were," Ray said, attempting to use his glamour upon her. He'd never used it on a ghost before, but it was worth a try.

"I cannot move on until you are punished for what you did to me." She pointed a pale finger at him. She was gaining power; he shouldn't have spoken to her. In fact, the glamour might have made things worse. When he said he wanted excitement, this wasn't the sort of excitement he had in mind. This was bad. He had to stop this before it spiraled further out of control.

"You can see her?" Lady Thornton stared at him wide-eyed.

Ray blinked a few times. "How could I not, when she's standing right in front of me?"

Lady Thornton shook her head. "This can't be real. Neither of you is real..."

"Run from him before it's too late." The ghost grasped Catherine's shoulder. She was becoming corporeal, but just acknowledging her wouldn't be enough for that. Even if she'd gotten a bit of magic from his glamour. The rotting stench grew stronger, and his stomach twisted. It wasn't just her desire for revenge that was keeping her tied to this plain. It was dark magic.

He put himself between the ghost and Lady Thornton. At this rate, a few more minutes and she'd would transform into a wraith, and he wasn't strong enough to fight her himself. She screeched as she lunged for him, clawing at him with hands so cold they burned. He wrestled with her, but she was stronger than he expected. Her rotting hand clenched around his windpipe, squeezing the air out of him.

"I just want this all to go away!" Catherine shouted. The

call of it reverberated toward him, slammed into his chest, burst from him like a lightning strike to earth, the echo of power shot outward and dislodged the ghost's grip around his throat.

Lady Thornton crouched on the ground, her knees drawn to her chest as she rocked back and forth. She muttered to herself under her breath. But he felt it, the tingle of power on her skin. It had flared out of her and into him. A tiny sliver of power swirled inside him, enough to summon his blade. He held out his hand, and a green vapor coalesced, forming into a short sword. Who was she?

The ghost gave a gurgling gasp. Black threads wound around the ghost's wrists, ankles, and throat, oozing like bleeding wounds. Frayed ends dangled as if they'd been severed. Whatever had been tethering her to the world of the living had been severed. Ray closed his fist and dismissed his blade. There was no use drawing it now. The ghost clutched at the frayed strings as it ran through her fingers, trying in vain to stop her power from escaping her.

Hooves clopped, and wooden wheels creaked. Death upon his midnight carriage parted the mist. His black stallions tossed their ebony manes and pawed the ground. Death beckoned for the ghost with a skeletal hand.

"No, you cannot take me. My business here is not complete. I have to protect Lady Thornton from him," she pleaded, hands clasped together.

He shook his hooded head and crooked his finger once more. The ghost rose up like a marionette and took a seat beside Death. The black stallions blew out a huff, and the wheels creaked as they pulled into the mist once more. As the carriage disappeared, the ghost glared back at him.

Lady Thornton had stopped rocking back and forth and stared blankly after the retreating carriage.

"Lady Thornton. It's alright now; the ghost has moved on." He gently shook her shoulders.

She recoiled from his touch. With her face averted, she stood.

"Pardon me, I should be going." She swayed on her feet, and he held out a hand to steady her, but she once more shrunk from his touch. Ray let his hand fall to his side.

It wouldn't be good to press her. She seemed to be in shock. Even those humans with the sight would be rattled by coming face to face with death themselves. But she wasn't merely a human, or a half breed; she had infused him with her power, by accident. It seemed he wouldn't be bored for a long time yet.

4

Catherine paced the length of her room, bare feet slapping on the hardwood floor as she circled her four-poster bed. Her untouched breakfast taunted her roiling stomach. Last night she'd slept in brief snatches. Each time she'd dozed off, she'd woken in a panic, expecting to be pulled from her bed. When Miss Larson had brought her breakfast, Catherine had given up the pretense of trying to sleep. This crawling anxiety wouldn't leave her since yesterday in the garden. The cold brush of the ghost's hands and the putrid smell of rot lingered in her nose like a foul perfume. As if her imagination had woven its way into the fabric of her clothing, her hair, under her nails, which she'd scrubbed and scrubbed until they were raw.

Rain drummed against the glass of her window. How long before Lord Thornton discovered the truth? How long before he sent her to Elk Grove as her parents had? If she returned, Dr. Armstrong would be furious. He would lock her in the room again. And this time, he wouldn't let her out. The dark oak panels on the walls closed in, and her chest constricted. She raced to the window and flung it open. The scent of wet earth wafted in, and she gulped in the cold air. The knot in her chest eased. This wasn't the room. She was free of Elk Grove. She would never go back. She'd come this far. Raindrops pattered on her hands as she clutched the windowsill. Her breaths escaped in short huffs. What was real? What was fake? Was the gardener, Mr. Thorn? Had she been in the garden at all yesterday? She was afraid to ask.

Normally a walk outside or burying her hands in earth would have calmed her nerves. But given the weather, that wasn't an option. At Elk Grove, walking about was forbidden, but here she was free to roam. Thornwood Abbey was sprawling, and there was an entire second wing she hadn't seen. Maybe if she just went for a walk, even indoors, it might dispel this restless energy. The door creaked as she eased it open onto a deathly silent hall. Lightning flashed and illuminated the area. Catherine flinched, half expecting to see a ghostly gaze staring at her from the shadows. But there was nothing but shadows cast by flickering candlelight, dark wood furnishings, and thick drawn curtains that hardly drowned out the pulsating torrent of rain on the windows.

On previous mornings, servants moved silently from room to room, heads down as they worked. But today, it was as if the entire house was abandoned. She scurried down the hall and paused along the landing that connected the west wing and the east. No one had forbidden her from going here. But Mrs. Morgan had made mention that most of this side of the house was boarded up. This side of the house was dark, the hall like a cavernous mouth opening into an endless void.

Lightning flashed again, illuminating the end of the hall and revealed portraits on the walls. Their hollow eyes glared at her. She yelped and took a step backward with one hand on the banister. Heart slamming into her rib cage, she looked around. There was nothing there but shadows. No ghosts with ominous warnings. No strange men with devilish smiles. Dr. Armstrong said to overcome her fears, she must confront them. If she didn't want to go back to Elk Grove, she had to prove to herself that there was nothing to fear. She removed a sconce from the wall. A delicate heat warmed her hand as she ventured into the darkness.

Dust tickled her nose, and she fought the urge to sneeze. The haunting gazes of the portraits followed her as she explored. Did Edward's ancestors watch her and find her wanting as his sister did? She was too afraid to look up and meet their empty eyes. Palms slick with sweat she grasped for the door knob. It groaned and swung open onto a bedroom shrouded in sheets. She coughed on the musty scent before closing the door again. That wasn't so bad.

A draft blew her candle out. Catherine looked back to the hall where she'd come, but it was cloaked in black. At the opposite end of the hall, a faint light glowed. Perhaps this wing of the house wasn't as abandoned as she had thought. Like a moth drawn to a flame, she darted for the open door. She eased it open to discover a nursery.

A south-facing window illuminated a buttery yellow nursery. The storm had passed, it seemed. Catherine inched closer to the window and peered through the rain-streaked grass. The forest loomed in the distance, veiled in shadows. The hairs on the back of her neck stood on end as she recalled the eerie song which had drawn her to it. She turned away and banged her knee on a rocking chair. Catherine hissed in pain and backed away from it, knocking over a pile of children's toys. She held up her hands, surveying the room for anymore tripping hazards. In a far corner sat a lonely bassinet.

Unlike the other room she'd found in this end of the wing, nothing had been covered up. Nor was there that musty smell or the dust on any surface. Someone had been keeping this room clean. But why a nursery of all things? Had Lord Thornton prepared it in anticipation of starting a family? She supposed it was the natural progression of a marriage. Yet they hadn't even consummated theirs. What sort of mother would she make? She'd dreamed of a family when she was at Elk Grove. A happy, uncomplicated life. She approached the bassinet, a single finger extended to caress the delicate lace that trimmed the rim of the bassinet.

"My lady, what are you doing here?" Mrs. Morgan's sharp tone sounded disapproving.

Catherine spun around to face her, dropping her hands to her sides as a blush burned her skin. Maybe she shouldn't have come here.

"I apologize. The candle blew out and then the door..." She bowed her head.

"I thought I told you, this wing of the house is boarded up. There's nothing for you here." Mrs. Morgan stepped out of the way, her arm extended to guide Catherine out.

"Yes, of course." She hurried to exit. But as she did, she couldn't help but glance once more back at the nursery. Mismatched furniture draped in sheets filled the room. Catherine pressed her palm to her mouth. Yellowed wallpaper peeling up in the corners covered the walls. A dusty bassinet and one broken leg sat in the corner. She shook her head. Had she imagined an entire room? Sunlight streamed through the window, mocking her.

"My lady?" Mrs. Morgan prompted.

"Coming." Catherine tore her gaze away and followed Mrs. Morgan down the hall between beams of sunlight pressing through the shuttered windows. The visions had never been this bad before, and they were becoming more vivid. Her thigh throbbed where she'd struck it on the rocking chair.

She needed to get out of this house, feel the wind against her face and the sun on her skin. Too long indoors always made her restless. That must be why the visions had gotten so bad. When she married Edward, she never thought being a lady would be quite so complicated. While Catherine might be a failure, Mrs. Morgan moved with surprising speed to prepare her for a walk. It took mere minutes to summon Miss Larson with Catherine's coat and boots and a second maid with a basket to deliver to Mrs. Rosewood—since she was going out anyway.

Basket slung over her arm, she stepped out onto the circular drive. Gravel crunched beneath her boots, and she inhaled the scent of damp soil. She took her time and enjoyed the gentle squish of mud under her boots as she strolled down the road. Shallow puddles had formed in the grooves left by carriage wheels, and frogs croaked nearby. The knot of tension in her chest loosened. Everything would be fine. She would be fine.

At the end of the lane, a low, stone wall encircled a small cottage with white siding and tall gray roofs. Ivy spilled out of pots on the front porch and dangled, covering the white banisters. Even if Mrs. Morgan hadn't given her directions, Catherine would have guessed it was Mrs. Rosewood's cottage. It exuded the same warm energy as its mistress. A wooden slatted gate opened onto an herb garden where bees buzzed, bouncing among dewdrop covered petals of early blooming flowers. In some of her darkest moments at Elk Grove, she imagined a life in a cozy cottage like this. Days spent working in her garden, a loving husband who would come home and swing her in his arms in greeting.

Catherine adjusted the weight of the basket and knocked on the green door.

The patter of footsteps preceded a muffled, "Coming." The door swung open. Mrs. Rosewood, wearing an apron with a pattern of flowers, answered the door. "Oh, Lady Thornton, what a pleasant surprise." She stepped aside to let Catherine inside.

The foyer was intimate but brightened by minty green wallpaper with a design of intertwining vines. A vase of yellow daffodils sat on the nearby credenza. It should have been too early for such blooms. There had been flowers on the table at dinner; perhaps Mrs. Rosewood had a greenhouse and provided them. She'd love to see it and ask her for her gardening secrets.

"Lord Thor— Edward, asked me to bring you a few things." Catherine held up her basket.

"Oh my, he is so thoughtful. Here let me take that from you. Will you stay for tea?" She unburdened Catherine with a smile.

"Yes, thank you."

Women's laughter escaped from behind the partially closed door. Mrs. Rosewood glanced toward it. "You're just in time. I was just about to bring out tea for my other guests. Please sit, and I'll join you momentarily." She nodded her head toward the room as she carried the basket toward the back of the cottage.

"Aunt, who is it?" Lydia poked her head into the foyer. She looked at Catherine and then back into the room beyond. A sly smile spread over her face. "Catherine, how wonderful to see you."

She wanted to run, but her feet were rooted to the spot. Lydia already had reason to not like her; she shouldn't add rudeness on top of it. If she wanted to overcome her fears, she had to face them. Lydia was disappointed that Edward hadn't married her best friend. But maybe they could still be friends if Catherine only tried.

Lydia twirled, throwing the door open wide. "Mary, this is her, the woman I was telling you about."

A pretty blond sat on the sofa. She had a flushed round face and sparkling blue eyes.

"It's lovely to meet you," she said as she stood to greet her.

"Catherine, this is Miss Ashton. I told you about her at dinner the other night." Lydia's smirk made Catherine's insides squirm. This was her, the woman Lydia hoped Edward would marry. If Edward was the hero of a novel, Miss Ashton looked like the perfect heroine. No wonder Lydia had wanted them to marry. They would have been an ideal match. Catherine twisted her hands together.

Her throat felt suddenly tight.

"Come sit with us," Lydia said as she plopped down on the sofa next to Miss Ashton and patted the seat opposite her.

Catherine dragged leaden feet over to the sofa. Under normal circumstances, she wasn't a great conversationalist. But sitting this close to Miss Ashton and seeing her dewy skin and perfect posture, she felt the curve of her slumping shoulders and her sickly pale skin stand out even more in contrast. She threaded her fingers together and rested them on her lap to keep herself from fidgeting.

"How are you enjoying Thornwood so far?" Miss Ashton asked.

"It is lovely," Catherine murmured.

"It must feel strange coming in as an outsider," said Lydia. "Mary and I have grown up with the foggy forests, and strange superstitions of the locals." She laughed, but Miss Ashton didn't join her. "Mary, remember that time I dared you to go into the woods, and you swore you saw a man there?" she asked Miss Ashton, shaking her head. Her body turned as if to box Catherine out.

CATHERINE'S HEAD PERKED UP, AND SHE STUDIED MISS Ashton. She'd seen a man in the woods? It must be a coincidence, surely.

Miss Ashton even blushed prettily as she stared at her folded hands. "I went missing overnight. My mother was so angry with me when they found me the next morning curled up in the roots of an old oak."

"Edward nearly lost his mind with worry. I remember he stayed out all night searching for you. Was that the night he got bit by that wild dog?" Lydia asked.

Miss Ashton laughed thinly. "Was it? I don't remember." She glanced toward Catherine, and when their eyes met, she jerked her head away to look out of the window instead.

"At least it wasn't a Thorn Dweller's moon." Lydia laughed harder, but she was the only one doing so.

Miss Ashton stared blankly outside, her face ashen. Catherine knew that expression all too well. She'd seen it on countless residents' faces at Elk Grove. What had Miss Ashton seen in the woods that night?

"What is a Thorn Dweller's moon?" Catherine asked,

curiosity getting the better of her. It felt dangerous to even wonder, when her visions had been so vivid lately.

"Oh, I suppose you wouldn't know about that coming from London, would you?" Lydia said with a triumphant expression.

"It's a village superstition. Back in the old days, everyone used to blame things on the fae. If milk turned sour, if your favorite dress got a tear. They were even convinced that the fae took children from their cribs." She shook her head. "But you don't believe in that nonsense, do you, Catherine?"

The hairs on the back of Catherine's neck stood on end. "Certainly not," she said it a bit too emphatically.

Miss Ashton met her gaze this time, and she didn't look away. Was she imagining things, or was that compassion in her eyes?

"Lydia, come help me. I fear I can't carry all the tea things myself!" Mrs. Rosewood called from the room beyond.

Lydia stood with a huff. "Really, Aunt. You should hire a maid for this sort of thing..." Her footsteps faded away, and it was just Catherine and Miss Ashton.

The grandfather clock against the far wall bonged the hour. When it finished, a yawning silence filled the room. Surely neither of them wanted to be in this situation, Edward's wife and presumably his past lover? What did Miss Ashton feel for Lord Thornton? As much as she wanted to know, she also feared the answer. If she discovered that they had been in love and had come between them, she wasn't sure she could forgive herself. If Edward were that inconstant, would he one day tire of her as well?

"I hope you don't think ill of Lydia. She means well," Miss Ashton said.

Catherine nodded. Her throat was too tight to speak.

"If I may give you advice?" Miss Ashton prompted.

Catherine's skin pebbled. "Yes?" she croaked.

"If you're ever out at night on a full moon and hear music." She hesitated; there was a crash somewhere in the house. Miss Ashton's wide eyes darted in that direction. Murmured voices; Lydia or Mrs. Rosewood must have dropped something. Miss Ashton scooted closer to Catherine. She could smell the hint of her lilac perfume.

Miss Ashton craned her neck to watch the door and then back to Catherine. "Be careful of the woods. Thornwood isn't like other villages. Strange things happen, things beyond belief."

Catherine's heart thundered in her chest. She thought of the ghost, the peculiar gardener, the doorway in the forest. The song which had lured her closer. It couldn't be real. She refused to believe it. The visions were getting worse; perhaps she was imagining this conversation as well.

"Really, Lydia, how could you be so clumsy," Mrs. Rosewood chided as she entered the parlor.

"This is why you need help," Lydia returned.

They were getting closer. "There isn't much time. I can't talk about it in front of others. They don't believe me. But tomorrow morning, meet me on the lane. There are things you must know about."

"I'm not an invalid. I can do this much myself," Mrs. Rosewood said as she entered the room. Her gaze swept over the two of them, and she smiled. "Oh. Isn't it lovely to see you two getting along? See, Lydia, there's no hard feelings."

Lydia huffed. "What could the two of them possibly have to talk about?"

Mrs. Rosewood handed Catherine and Miss Ashton each

a cup of tea. Though her hands shook, Catherine lifted her own cup off the saucer and spilled the scalding liquid onto her hand.

Mrs. Rosewood leaped to dab at it with a handkerchief. "Catherine, are you hurt?"

"I'm fine," she said automatically. Her eyes were drawn once more to Miss Ashton, who shook her head slowly. Her intention clear. Don't speak. But did that mean Miss Ashton saw them too?

5

Catherine peered through the crack in the grand oak doors. Edward leaned on his elbow. The top buttons of his shirt were undone, and his collar flipped up. He ran a hand through his disheveled hair and frowned at the document on his dark mahogany desk. If she interrupted, would he be angry? Dr. Armstrong hated it when she disturbed his work. But she and Edward were married. She should try and make an effort, shouldn't she? What if he changed his mind and decided to annul their marriage? They'd yet to consummate it after all... Edward sighed heavily, and Catherine jerked back from the crack in the door. Back pressed against the wall, she exhaled.

Her confidence in Edward had wavered since meeting Miss Ashton. Who was she to compare to a woman of such poise and kindness? Why would Edward choose Catherine over her? Had their families forbade the match? No. That wasn't possible. Lydia made that much clear, and she doubted Miss Ashton's family wouldn't have been thrilled to have a lord for a son-in-law. Did Miss Ashton love another? But if that were true, why had Miss Ashton looked so sad?

When dawn had risen after yet another sleepless night, Catherine had resolved to not meet with her. Pretending the problem didn't exist was infinitely easier. Besides, she had an inkling of what Miss Ashton wanted to tell her. "Edward had been in love with me, but fate kept us apart; please give him up." Catherine shook her head. Perhaps not something quite so melodramatic. The alternative was that Miss Ashton had something more to tell her about the forest, about that strange gate and the peculiar things she'd witnessed since she'd arrived here. She wasn't sure which was worse. That all of that was real, or she had torn apart two people in love to stay out of the madhouse.

A gust of wind blew down the hall, and she shuddered. She glanced along the empty passage. A cluster of anemones drooped in their vase atop the credenza. There was no use disturbing Edward right now.

"Catherine! Now, this is a pleasant surprise," Edward called.

The wind had blown the door open and exposed her hiding spot. Catherine's face flushed.

"Pardon me, I did not mean to disturb you. I can come back later." Catherine addressed the floor. She turned on her heel.

He grasped her by the wrist. She tensed and yanked her hand away. He wasn't going to punish her, was he? She never should have come here. Edward was an important man, and she'd wasted his time on her insignificant feelings. She turned to face him wide-eyed, one hand clenching the fabric at her throat. Edward canted his head to the side as he furrowed his brows.

Her blush only deepened. This wasn't Elk Grove. Edward wasn't going to lock her away in the room for misbehaving. He wasn't Dr. Armstrong.

"You can visit me whenever you like; there's no need for apologies." Edward smiled again, but it didn't quite reach his eyes.

Dark smudges darkened under his eyes, and a yellow tea stain marred his white shirt. When had he changed his clothes last, or ate a proper meal? He seemed to hardly ever leave his study. Instead of wasting his time with her, he should be resting. Catherine pulled down the hem of her sleeve and rubbed the silken fabric between thumb and forefinger.

"Did you have something to ask me?" Edward prompted.

"Oh. Well..." She hadn't thought that far ahead. "The thing is, we haven't seen much of one another." She winced. Now she sounded like Mama nagging at Papa.

"You're right. I feel as if we have barely had a moment to speak since we've arrived home. Perhaps we can go for a walk about the garden together. You can tell me your plans for it."

Catherine's head shot up. "Are you sure? You seemed to have more demanding matters to attend to." Her eyes drifted to his desk, cluttered with papers, and then back to him.

"My work will still be there when I get back. Let me just ring for my coat, and we can head out." He reached for the pull cord on the wall, and a distant bell rang. And then he turned back to her with another smile. She wanted to reach out and wipe away the smear of ink on his chin. That was the sort of affectionate gesture a wife would do. Her finger twitched. If she did, would he push her away or pull her closer and...

Edward cleared his throat. "Mrs. Morgan says preparations are underway for the ball."

"Yes. I believe so." Just this morning, Mrs. Morgan had delivered choices for invitations; the supposed varying shades of creme paper had all looked the same to her, and so she'd picked one at random. The thought of the ball made her chest tight. She prayed she didn't embarrass Edward in front of his friends and neighbors. She couldn't dance and had not the faintest clue how to host such an event.

The door to the study flew open, and Catherine jumped back, colliding with Edward, who caught her shoulders. She pressed her arms to her side. Edward let her go without a word. But he must realize now she recoiled from unexpected touch. It evoked memories of the grasping hands of the caretakers at Elk Grove.

"My Lord, it happened again! The prize hogs are all slaughtered, and Mr. Moore is—" He looked up, and his thick mustache sagged. "I didn't realize you had company." He removed his bowler hat and clutched it in tanned and chaffed hands.

"Ah, yes. Mr. Wolfe, this is my wife, Lady Thornton." Edward gestured toward her.

Mr. Wolfe bobbed his head in greeting. "Pleasure, my lady. Lord Thornton has spoken highly of you."

Catherine bobbed her head in greeting.

"Mr. Wolfe is my estate manager. I don't know what I'd do without the man," Edward said with a strained smile.

Mr. Wolfe nodded beneath his praises though his smile was stiff as well. He and Edward exchange a furtive look. There was something neither of them was saying. Dr.

Armstrong and the nurses at Elk Grove did the same. It usually preceded her being locked in the room. Ice ran through her veins.

"I must see to this. There's a wild dog on the loose, you see. It's been killing my tenant farmer's livestock. And the beasts are costing me dearly. We've yet to catch the thing." Edward sighed and rubbed his hand over his face. "I am sorry, Catherine, we'll have to walk together another time." He reached toward her, and she noticed dirt embedded in his nail beds and the grains of his palms. He pulled back at the last moment as if second-guessing himself.

"I understand," Catherine said as her shoulders slumped.

"Give us a moment, will you, Mr. Wolfe?" Edward said.

Mr. Wolfe nodded as he put on his bowler hat. He left, closing the door after him. The click of the door made her stomach flop, and she glanced toward the window facing the garden. Using the swaying branches of the forest like an anchor. This wasn't the room. Catherine fidgeted with the hem of her sleeve. Edward wouldn't harm her. She wanted to believe that. But she couldn't shed fear like it was a coat. How long before he gave up on trying to hold out a hand to her altogether?

"I'm sorry to do this to you. I promise I will make it up to you somehow." His wrinkled brow and down turned mouth didn't suit his handsome face.

She shouldn't be causing trouble for him. Not after what he'd done for her and her family. "Don't trouble yourself over me; the tenants need you."

"How about this, tomorrow you and I will go for a ride in my two-seater." He flashed her a smile. Now he resembled the gentleman she'd met in London.

Her stomach fluttered. "I would like that very much." Her face flushed for an entirely different reason.

He leaned in slowly, and this time she forced herself to stay very still as he planted a kiss on her forehead. It was warm and soft. When he pulled away, her stomach was doing somersaults. "I look forward to it then."

Even after he left, Catherine continued to stare at the empty doorway. Elk Grove had left its mark on her, but if they took it slow and Edward was willing to be patient, maybe she could learn to be more like a heroine. She wiped her clammy hands on her skirt, but she couldn't wipe the smile from her face. Miss Larson, her lady's maid, arrived with her coat slung over her arm.

"You're in fine spirits," Miss Larson remarked as she held up Catherine's coat for her.

"Am I?" Catherine tried to contain her smile. Her heart danced about her rib cage.

"Something good happen?" Miss Larson prompted with a cheeky smile.

She couldn't contain herself and replied, "Lord Thornton asked me to go for a ride in his two-seater tomorrow."

Miss Larson chuckled as she tied the ribbon of Catherine's bonnet under her chin. "You'd think you were lovers rather than husband and wife."

Catherine pressed a hand to her flushed cheek. Is that what they looked like? There had been brief moments like this during their courtship, but they'd been overshadowed by her desperation to marry. She didn't have the luxury of love. It was either wed or go back to Elk Grove, and Edward had asked, so she had agreed. Was this what it felt like to be in love? It felt different than in stories.

Dressed and ready, Catherine headed out for her morning

walk. Thick fog blanketed the front drive, and she couldn't see beyond the reach of her arm. The last time she'd been in fog this thick, she thought she saw the ghost. The crunch of her boots on gravel echoed around her, and she pulled her coat tighter to her chest. Should she head back inside? A shadow darted along the periphery of her vision. Catherine did a double take. A birch tree's branches waved in the faint breeze. Her eyes were playing tricks on her again. Nothing to be scared of. This was her fresh start. Ignore it. Pretend you don't see.

She stuck to the road and headed toward the village instead of walking the manor grounds. A voice whispered the words. No. It had to be the wind through the trees. A hand grasped the hem of her skirt. She spun around only to find it had gotten caught on some shrubbery she'd wandered too close to. Miss Ashton's words floated in her mind: *Thornwood isn't like other villages. Strange things happen, things beyond belief.* Her arm pebbled, and she rubbed it. There was nothing to be worried about. It was village superstition like Lydia said. Nothing could hurt her if it were all in her head. A bare foot protruded from behind a stone wall. A chill crept up her spine. That couldn't be. Cautiously, she approached. She rubbed her eyes. It must be a pale rock...

The leg attached to that foot disappeared beneath the tattered and dirt-stained skirt. A dark red stain spread out across the bodice of the lilac gown. Blood seeped from the gaping hole where her chest had been cut open. Golden hair fanned out across the gravel, and blue eyes stared sightlessly at the sky. A body. Miss Ashton.

A scream caught in her throat as Catherine stumbled backward. She covered her eyes and fell into a crouch on the ground as she rocked back and forth. She couldn't catch her breath. She gasped for each breath as her heart beat hard enough to burst from her chest, her pulse pounded in her neck, thundered in her ears. Not real. Not real. Not real...

She couldn't open her eyes. But when she opened her eyes, it would be gone. It would be another hallucination. She cracked open an eye. It hadn't changed. Miss Ashton's blood soaked into the gravel; one foot still had a shoe on, the other had cuts in the sole. When they met yesterday, she'd been wearing that dress. Catherine covered her mouth in a failed attempt to hold back the bile that clawed at the back of her throat. She crawled to the side of the road, where she expelled her breakfast.

TREMBLING, SHE CHECKED FOR THE THIRD TIME. NOTHING had changed. Miss Ashton was dead. What did she do? Should she alert a constable? She wasn't sure she could stand up without tipping over. A hand fell on her shoulder. A scream ripped out of her, and she picked up a rock chucking it at her assailant. The killer was still here. She would be next. The ghost tried to warn her, but she hadn't listened.

"Lady Thornton, are you hurt?" Mr. Thorn held his hands up.

Catherine backed into the shrub, the branches stabbing into her back. Her hands clawed in the dirt, searching for a weapon, anything to defend herself with. The ghost warned her. She said Mr. Thorn would take her heart. But ghosts weren't real. And yet. Miss Ashton's glassy eyes stared upward. She needed to run, get back to the manor. Her hand scrabbled for a rock that filled her palm. She wasn't sure of her aim, but it was worth a shot.

He stalked closer, hands outstretched, she lobbed the rock. It sailed right past him.

"Stay back!" Catherine screeched.

He paused, brow furrowed. "You don't have to be afraid of me. I saw you collapse..."

"Was it you?" She pointed a shaking hand toward the body on the ground. His eyes followed where her finger pointed. A part of her feared his gaze would skim right over it. But his gaze rested there, and his skin paled as his eyes widened.

"No. Not again," he said so softly she could barely hear him.

"Can you see it?" Catherine croaked. She couldn't tear her gaze away. This wasn't another vision. It was real. Her empty stomach heaved, and she wretched again, but nothing came up. It was real. Miss Ashton was dead?

"The body, yes..." He shook his head, turning his gaze away from it. Miss Ashton's body...Catherine swayed. This couldn't be real. When all the other times it hadn't been real, why now? She couldn't tear her gaze away from the broken, bloody nails, the dirt smeared on her skirt. Her vision swam.

"Lady Thornton, we need to get you home." Mr. Thorn put himself between her and the body.

He offered his hand once more to help her up. Her arms were too weak to lift. Her entire body felt light. She shook her head. Her vision blurred as Mr. Thorn said something that she couldn't hear. She pitched forward as everything went black.

6

Ray lurched to catch Lady Thornton before her skull cracked upon on the ground. He cradled her fragile body in his arms. No matter how long he spent among them, humans continued to surprise him. One moment they were lobbing rocks at your head, the next, their emotions overwhelmed them, and they collapsed. The air reeked of blood. At first, he had thought it had been Lady Thornton's. Until the acrid scent of aberrant magic hit him. All magic flowed from the Great Tree and brought life to both the human realm and the other realm. For that magic to be used to kill, it tainted not only the wielder but the very ground where the sacrilege had occurred.

The high courts had banned blood magics and curses centuries ago. The risks far outweighed the rewards. But the fae were greedy, and he'd heard whispers of maiden hearts and their potent magic, especially when human and fae blood mixed. His lip curled.

That ghost had the same done to her, and then her soul bound by dark magic. This girl did not seem as unfortunate as the first, but it was a troubling pattern. Thornwood had been quiet until now. Until Lady Thornton arrived and stumbled upon the gateway. It could be a coincidence, or it could be a portent of ruin. Either way, he wasn't about to get tangled up in wicked dealings.

Lady Thornton had yet to regain consciousness, and he couldn't just leave her lying on the side of the road. He'd deliver her to Thornwood Abbey and wash his hands of her and these murders. He lifted her up into his arms. Her head lolled like a rag doll, and he rested it against his shoulder. The feather-soft strands of her hair brushed against his cheek. The skin of her eyelids was translucent, and the blue of her veins stood out stark against her fair skin. Thick, black lashes brushed the tops of her pale cheeks.

"You're too much trouble for me, I'm afraid, Lady Thornton," he said as he shifted her weight to make sure he didn't lose grip of her amidst all the layers of fabric. How human women moved about beneath such bulk was beyond him.

The fog rolled away as he headed down the road. A hazel tree's branches sagged beneath the weight of a snowy owl. Its golden eyes watched him approach unblinking. It was much too early for her to be out hunting. He passed under the tree, and around the bend, the iron gate of Thornwood Abbey came into view. Normally he'd avoid going near it, but it was the most direct route back. And the sooner he unloaded his burden, the better.

The snowy owl took flight, gliding above him, and landed atop a cypress tree lining the drive up the front of the manor. Ray met its gaze as he passed. The owl flashed a brief grin. They'd dropped their glamour for a silent hello or perhaps a taunt. If the snowy owl was the killer, they might be trying to establish their territory, that or looking for their next victim.

Lady Thornton frowned in sleep but did not stir further. Not his business.

Ray whistled to himself, in part to ignore the snowy owl, but also to hide from Mr. Rockwell. It was an ineffective cloaking spell. The sound would project his voice and hopefully lure Mr. Rockwell in the opposite direction. If they crossed paths, however, Ray wasn't sure he could explain away an unconscious Lady Thornton. Away from the forest, his magic weakened. Normally it lasted from moon to moon. But it was taking more and more to keep Mr. Rockwell docile. When he'd left this morning, he intended not to return until after the full moon when his power would be restored. Just a few more days, and he could resume his duty at the gateway.

The owl hooted as Mr. Rockwell came stomping around the corner. His face was a bright plum, and his hands were balled into fists. Ray tightened his grip on Lady Thornton, and she groaned. A prickling sensation raced down his spine, and a rush of magic flooded his body.

Mr. Rockwell turned his head and pointed at Ray. "You!" he growled.

He stormed over.

"You cannot see me; you will forget I exist until after the full moon," Ray said in a rush, his tongue tingling with magic.

Mr. Rockwell halted his steps, his expression blank, and his jaw slack. He looked around the garden, his gaze sliding over Ray as if he hadn't seen him at all.

It had really worked. He didn't know how it did, but it had. In his arms, Lady Thornton stirred. She heaved a sigh and buried her face against his chest. *Who are you?* Fae had taken human lovers throughout both their long histories.

Never before had he seen a product of one of these unions have the sort of latent powers Lady Thornton possessed. Curious. He shook his head. It was none of his business. Death shadowed her. He wasn't prepared to get mixed in another human's affairs. He'd made that mistake once and never again.

They reached the door to the kitchen. Ray shouldered it open. Cook shouted at her assistant and didn't notice him sneak past. At the end of the hall, a staircase led up to the main part of the house. Beyond here, there was too much iron and old wards that seeped into the walls and made his skin twitch. In and out. Drop her in a bedroom and be on his way. They'd gotten this far thanks to the glamour, but the iron and wards stripped it away like a river erodes the bank. Up the stairs and sweat beaded his brow. Lady Thornton, who'd been light as a feather before now felt like a sack of rocks. His breaths were labored as he assessed the closed door with its damned iron knob. Touching it would burn, and there were more obstacles waiting within.

"Where are you going?" Came a sour voice from the bottom of the steps.

Ray sighed and turned and revealed Lady Thornton. The housekeeper's mouth fell slack.

What was her name? Mrs. Thompson? No. She'd been a housekeeper twenty or fifty years ago. Not Mrs. Moore, she was a reedy woman blind in one eye.

"What is the meaning of this? What have you done to Lady Thornton?" She rushed forward, pressing her finger under Lady Thornton's nose. Now he remembered. This one was Mrs. Morgan. She always watched him with narrowed eyes when he snuck into the kitchen. She asked a lot of inconvenient questions about his work. Some humans were more observant than others, and those that saw easily through glamours he avoided.

The other servants must have heard the commotion and gathered in the hallway. Cook arrived and wiped her hands on her apron. The butler poked his bald head from his office a few feet from him. Servants whispered amongst themselves. He shifted Lady Thornton's increasing weight in his arms. If it weren't for them, he would have attempted the glamour despite the iron. But he wasn't strong enough to glamour them all, not even with Lady Thornton's unwitting help.

"I found her collapsed outside; I think she fainted," he said crisply to the housekeeper.

The servants tittered, looking at one another wide-eyed. The housekeeper's eyes widened for a brief second. It was the only indication she had heard what he'd said at all. Humans were quick to make up fanciful imaginings. When the body was discovered, Ray would be the first one they pointed the finger to. It was a damned shame; he hoped to get another decade out of this persona.

"Mr. Fox, take Lady Thornton to her room," Mrs. Morgan said to a man standing in the hallway behind her.

A man in black and white stepped forward and held out his hands to Ray as if he were going to receive a sack of soil.

"Are you planning on slinging her over your shoulder?" Ray sneered.

The man flushed and shook his head as Ray carefully eased Lady Thornton into the other man's arms, making sure her head didn't contort at a strange angle. He watched the man take Lady Thornton up the stairs. What was he doing? This wasn't his problem. She was back with the humans, and that should be the end of it.

"Well, then." Ray dusted his hands together.

"One moment, I have a few more questions for you. Come to my office," the housekeeper said.

She gestured for him to join her in a small room just off the hall. The longer he lingered this close to iron, the weaker he would become. He might end up crawling out of here. But if he refused, it might only make her more suspicious. Leather-bound books and neat piles of papers filled an oak desk. On the corner, a kettle and steaming cup awaited beside an open book with lines of scrawled notes.

"Back to work, everyone. We've dinner to prepare," Mrs. Morgan said as she closed the door after him.

Ray stood on shaking legs. With sweat-slicked hands, he tugged at the collar of his shirt. It did little to ease the constricting feeling in his throat. Each scrap of iron in the walls, to the nails in the desk and chairs, pulsed in his blood and made him sluggish. It would take days locked in here to do any permanent damage, but he would be weak for hours after leaving.

"Have a seat.'" She gestured at a leather-bound chair with iron buttons running along the arms. He wasn't going anywhere near that chair. She took a seat herself and folded her hands in front of her, and met his gaze. There was something unsettling about her stare, or maybe it was the slow poison of the iron, because his stomach heaved.

"I'm a rather busy man; what is this about?" Ray said and hid his trembling hands behind his back.

"I'll keep myself brief then. What you saw today, I want you to keep it to yourself." She folded her hands on her desk in front of her.

What was she trying to insinuate? He hadn't even mentioned the body. "Can I ask why?" he said.

"Lord Thornton has a certain reputation to uphold, as does the rest of Thornwood Abbey. It would be best if you did not speak out of turn about this." She fixed him with her gaze once more.

He felt the faintest crackle of energy. Was she trying to use a glamour upon him? But she wasn't fae, he was certain of that. Ray sniffed the room, and it smelled faintly of herbs. Around her, he could see the faint outline of a thread, likely some sort of charm. A hedge witch. He'd never noticed before, but then again, he'd never paid that much attention. But if she were inclined to wipe his memory rather than ask a question, he was more than willing to play along.

He slackened his expression and said, "I understand," in a droning monotone of someone ensorcelled.

She leaned back with a faint smile. "Good, you are dismissed."

Ray showed himself out into the hall. A few staff members scurried away from the door where they'd likely been eavesdropping. Would she wipe their memories to keep Lady Thornton's fainting a secret? Humans were funny creatures. He'd gotten away easily this time, but once that body was discovered, he doubted he would be as lucky. Something should be done, he supposed. Ray gave a heavy sigh. His work never ended, it seemed.

<hr />

Something damp rested on Catherine's forehead. A single drop rolled over her temple. With leaden arms, Catherine reached up to bat it away. When had she fallen asleep? She blinked up at the draped purple velvet canopy.

Where was she? Sunlight streamed in from a window, and she screwed her eyes shut. Her thoughts moved like mud.

"Is she coming to?" Edward asked. He sounded panicked Catherine squinted and saw Mrs. Rosewood and Edward staring down at her.

"Don't crowd, let her breathe," Mrs. Rosewood said with her hand on Edward's shoulder.

They stepped back from her bedside. Catherine blinked, taking in the room. The vanity with the bottles of perfume and hair oils, the privacy screen with the painting of a tranquil countryside, and on the nightstand a bowl of water a rag slung over the rim. Her room at Thornwood Abbey.

Her head felt full of cotton, and connecting was like stumbling in the dark. How had she gotten into bed? The last she'd seen Edward had been in his study. Then she'd gone to take a walk; she recalled the crisp air. The thick banks of fog. A pale foot, a bloody dress, a gash in Miss Ashton's chest where her heart had been.

Catherine shot up. The damp cloth on her forehead slid off and fell into her lap with a wet plop.

"Miss Ashton. Someone—" Catherine's throat tightened. She couldn't say the words. It was too late. Miss Ashton was dead. She clamped her hand to her mouth. She'd seen a dead body. It had been real this time. Mr. Thorn had seen it as well. But who would have done such a horrid thing?

Edward took a seat on the edge of her bed with brow furrowed. "Catherine, darling, what are you talking about?" He reached to grasp her hand, but she pulled back on instinct. He blinked at her before resting his hands in his lap.

"Does your head hurt? Mrs. Morgan said they found you after you fainted on your morning walk. If only I had joined you, this wouldn't have happened."

67

She shook her head. Her mouth felt so dry. "Miss Ashton, she's been—" Catherine swallowed hard. She had seen it. Miss Ashton's vacant blue eyes were burned into her memory. If the ghost reappeared, would it have Miss Ashton's face? Looming in the shadows and issuing dire warnings.

Edward turned to Mrs. Rosewood. "Why would she be talking about Mary? They've never met."

"But I did. Just yesterday when I delivered the basket to Mrs. Rosewood," Catherine said, looking to Mrs. Rosewood for confirmation. She should have told Edward when she had the chance. What if she had gone to meet Miss Ashton, would she have suffered the same fate?

Edward shook his head. "Miss Ashton has been in London for months. There is no way you would have met her."

"But I—" What was the use in arguing. It had all felt so real. She thought for certain this time that it wasn't another hallucination. Her eyes darted between Mrs. Rosewood and Edward as they exchanged a look. Surely Mrs. Rosewood would corroborate her story.

"The other day when Catherine came to visit, Lydia was causing trouble again. You know how she is. She kept bringing up Miss Ashton..."

Catherine's heart stuttered. No. Mrs. Rosewood was there, and so was Lydia. And Mr. Thorn had seen the body. She saw ghosts and from time to time—strange creatures. She didn't imagine encounters with women she'd never met, and she didn't make up gruesome murders.

"Perhaps we should call Dr. Rowan back?" Edward said.

They would send her away. Lock her up in a room, and she'd never see the light again. She reached for Edward, grasping his hand. "It's nothing. Forgive me, I must have hit my head when I fainted. It's like Mrs. Rosewood said, I got confused because of Lydia's teasing." Her voice was shrill, but she didn't care. As long as they didn't call a doctor.

He would see she had been telling lies. He would punish her. Tears threatened the back of her lids, but she clamped down on the rising feelings of hysteria. That only made the punishment worse. Her pulse galloped as it pounded in her neck. Screams filled her ears, and Catherine had to force herself to hold onto Edward, to not try and clamp her hands over her ears in an attempt to block them out. Then he would know. He would see that she was mad, and it would all be over.

Edward sat back down on the bed beside her and grasped her shoulder. "Are you certain?"

"I am." Her voice was a mere thread. Her bottom lip trembled. Surely he would see through her lies. Everything would be exposed. But more than anything, she wanted him to comfort her, to hold onto her, and tell her everything was going to be alright. To assure her, she wasn't mad.

A knock at the door proceeded Mrs. Morgan. "My Lord, a moment?"

Edward looked to Catherine and then squeezed her shoulder. "I'll be back soon."

He pulled away. As desperately as she wanted him to stay and comfort her, she dared not ask. She drew her knees up to her chest and wrapped her arms around them. She lowered her head, so she was in a tight ball. Just like Mama and Papa before him, Edward would cast her aside. No one wanted a broken girl.

"Catherine?" The words so softly spoken like a spell,

seeped into her cocoon of protection. "You're safe now; there's nothing to fear," she said.

Mrs. Rosewood hovered at the edge of her bed with a compassionate smile. So many times locked in that tiny dark room, she'd wished for someone to come and rescue her. She cried for the small folk to take her to Faery, for Mama and Papa to forgive her for being born wrong. But no one came. They never came.

Mrs. Rosewood took a seat on the edge of the bed, giving her plenty of space. But close enough that a hint of her lilac perfume wafted toward Catherine. It felt warm and comforting, and it tugged at a memory she couldn't quite place.

"Catherine, if you need someone to confide in, you can trust me. I'm sure coming to a new strange place can be scary."

How desperate she was to unburden herself onto Mrs. Rosewood in that moment. But Dr. Armstrong had been the same at first. Kind smile, gentle words until he changed. As kind and as compassionate as Mrs. Rosewood might seem, Catherine couldn't share this secret. She would do as she always had and pretend it hadn't happened at all.

7

Someone had removed the body. No. More than that, they'd erased all traces of it. Ray ran his hand through his hair, scratching his scalp as he studied the stone wall that lined the roadway. She'd been lying just there. You didn't see a body mutilated and easily forget. But not a drop of blood remained, nor a bent blade of grass or gore-soaked earth, which had been here prior. He'd walked between Thornwood Abbey to the Fairy Bride half a dozen times now and couldn't catch even the faintest scent of tainted magic. Only the sour stench of vomit where Lady Thornton had retched. It should have been a relief that someone had done his work for him. But this was too tidy.

A shadow darted through the trees beyond the wall. The forest encircled the village. Caught in an endless battle with humanity to tame it, the forest continued to push back. Roots crumbled walls, clumps of grass grew along the roadways, and heavy limbs draped over roofs and scattered fallen leaves into their yards. There were plenty of places to hide. Mist swirled about the trunks, and the branches of oak and ash swayed gently in the breeze. Whoever had done this, they'd done well to cover their tracks. Ray was the only loose end left to tie up.

He squatted down and reached for the bone dagger strapped to his ankle. The weight of a weapon in his hand was a comforting reassurance. If only it weren't just before the full moon, when he was at his weakest. He stood and turned slowly in a circle, eyes scanning. A twig snapped, and he pivoted toward it, readjusting the grip on the handle. Shadows greeted him. He crept closer to the woods. Blood magics were forbidden. Any caught practicing were severely punished, but few had the power to cover their kills. If he captured one that strong, it could be the bargaining chip he needed to leverage against the counsel.

The owl screeched as it burst from behind the mist. Ray swung his blade as it swooped overhead and landed on a nearby branch. He turned toward it, bone dagger poised.

"So it was you then," Ray said. He should have known when he caught her following him earlier.

It tilted its head to the side as it examined him with liquid golden eyes.

"Did you think hunting here would go unnoticed?" Ray lunged for the owl, but before he could strike, it took to the air and landed on a higher branch on a tree behind him.

"Is your rude tongue the reason you were exiled?" the owl responded. Her voice was that of a young woman, though many of his kind used different voices to trick their prey.

It knew him. That was unexpected, but mattered not. Whatever true form she might be, he would bind her and deliver her to the counsel. At the very least, they might take a few centuries off his punishment for capturing a practitioner of forbidden magics. Both courts low and high, had tried to snuff out the practice.

"You're quick to pass judgment when you are the one who has broken the accords." Ray's gaze shifted around him. She had the high ground. If only he could lure her down to him somehow.

She clicked her beak, and a sound akin to a laugh escaped her. "You should be thanking me for cleaning up this mess rather than making accusations. What would you have done when the humans found the body?"

He forced a laugh. "Do you really expect me to believe that you didn't kill that girl? Who else could it have been? There are no other fae in the human realm. Believe me, I would know."

The fae could disguise their true faces from humans and, to an extent, glamour themselves from one another. But there were always tells, subtle clues that gave them away. Not since the druids and ancient bone witches of centuries gone by had there been any use of the old magics in the human realm, which meant it had to be another fae.

"I don't know who killed those girls, only that I was ordered to clean up the mess." She stretched a wing and shifted from foot to foot. She tilted her head from side to side as she spoke in a parody of a stretch. "It's hard to get out the taint of abhorrent magic. We're fortunate it didn't leave an indelible mark upon the earth."

Either she was telling the truth, or she thought him an enormous fool. He wasn't certain anymore. "Why would you do that then, if it's so much trouble?"

She fixed him with her golden gaze. "Because the High Chancellor ordered me to do so. I believe his exact words were, 'Follow him and make sure he doesn't bring shame upon my name.'" She lowered her voice in a mockery of Father's.

Father was having him watched? And worse, he thought he'd bring further shame to him? When Father had exiled him, he had made it clear he wanted nothing more to do with him. How long had he been spied upon unawares? Ray had grown too complacent. The owl might not be the only one watching, if he knew Father.

"What makes him think I did this?" Ray asked.

She ruffled her feathers. "That's not the question you should be asking. You should be asking who did do it."

He shook his head. "This is none of my business. Thanks for taking care of the mess." He waved and turned to stride away. She swooped down onto the wall in front of him.

"It is true that I have seen you commit no crimes. But do you think your father's enemies will believe that? When they can use you to tear him down?"

Ray clenched his jaw. It shouldn't have mattered. Father had quickly covered up the mess. But he had a sinking feeling that this wasn't over, merely the beginning. Blood magic was old, as ancient as the great tree. These rituals were not taken on lightly. A single rite created a craving in the caster. As the hunger grew, they would kill again and again, never sated until it consumed them. Twice. Two women. And the first woman had pointed her finger at him. He thought it a coincidence, but if Father had sent someone to cover up the second. It could be no mere coincidence. There was no choice then. He had to find the killer before they struck again.

"Your father would see you," the owl said gravely.

Now wasn't today full of surprises. The owl swooped toward the forest. Ray hesitated to follow. Father would never lower himself as to leave Faery and enter the human realm, but he had been exiled on pain of death if he were to return. The mist swirled where the owl had passed through.

"Coming?" came her disembodied voice.

He clenched the leather grip of his bone dagger as he stepped into the forest. The owl screeched as she flew toward a slender oaken door. On it, a swirling pattern of interlocking rings forming a knot bristling with thorns had been burned into the wood. Father's sigil. The door creaked and opened onto Father's study. Wood shelves brimming with scrolls of parchment lined the wall. A fire crackling with green flames cast a green glow onto the smooth marble slab of his father's desk. The desk sat on the gnarled roots of an ancient oak from his family estate.

Home. He thought he'd never see it again. Even this brief glimpse brought with it a pang of longing. Father glanced up, his brows furrowed. Ray lingered at the threshold. Would he invite him inside? He dared not push his luck. Father set down the scroll he had been scowling at and stepped around his desk. Light from the fire limed golden bracers on his arms in emerald light. A golden circlet of branches with a ruby inset in the center circlet flickered and glared at him like an all-seeing eye from his brow.

"Raethorn," he said with the slightest incline of his head.

Rather than inviting Ray into his study, he stepped through the portal and joined Ray in the human realm. The oaken doors slammed shut behind him. Just like Father to give him a taste of the familiar and then twist the knife this way.

"Glad to know you still care enough to leave spies to watch over me," Ray said by way of greeting. Better to get this over with quickly.

"You have not changed at all in your time in exile, I see." Father's lip curled upward.

"What can I say? I'm my father's son."

"And that is the very reason I left Tabitha to watch over you."

Tabitha? A very human name. Unless. He looked at the owl perched on the nearby branch. She was preening her feathers. He could see it now, a changeling child used as a spy in the human realm. That was cruel, even for Father. Children stolen from the human realm and raised in Faery often took on fae-like qualities, but they were never fully human. Her owl form must be father's doing. He'd never been the nurturing type. Not since Mother died. And considering the way they'd parted all those years ago, he doubted he'd sent his spy out of fatherly concern.

"Were you hoping to catch me doing something you could execute me for, rather than just exile?" Ray asked.

"You're fortunate you are of my blood, or the council would have done much worse to you for what you did," his father said in a biting tone.

"You're right; I should be grateful the great and powerful regent turned his back upon me and let me take the fall for a human's treachery."

"Enough." Father's voice cracked with thunder, and the earth trembled under Ray's feet. Father must truly be angry then.

They glared at one another.

"I didn't call you here to squabble. I must give you a warning. If another girl dies, I cannot protect you again. I've taken all the precautions I can, but the counsel is restless."

"You seem rather certain it will happen again. Is there something you're not telling me?" This couldn't be the council's doing. What use would they have for attacking the regent's exiled son? It made no sense.

"Nothing I can say out in the open." His gaze flicked furtively around them as if the forest had eyes. Which if this were faery, it would have. But this was the human realm; nothing happened here. Well, that was until women started being murdered.

"And so? They've clearly been able to cover their tracks. How do you know they won't cover up a third?"

Father shook his head. "It's more than that. These women were chosen for a purpose. They had fae blood."

"How do you know that?" Ray asked.

"I have my ways." Father's expression was stony. There was no use trying to extract answers when he didn't want to give them.

But who would be killing women with fae blood? And to what end?

"Surely your spies can watch the gateways, track their movements. You're the regent, after all. You have the power to stop them," Ray said.

Father looked around them, dark eyes scanning the misty forest. "This isn't fae doing. Whoever it is, they are living in the human realm. Perhaps a human themselves."

"Impossible," Ray scoffed.

"Is it? A human killed our king, after all."

Ray flinched at the subtle jab. Father was right. If Ray hadn't trusted *her*, then he wouldn't be in this mess. He'd underestimated humans before. And he swore to himself, he wouldn't do so again.

"Find out by the next new moon."

A cold chill went down Ray's spine. A little over two weeks. That's all the time he had to find the killer?

"And if I don't?"

"Then it will be up to council to decide your fate." He tipped his head, and with a wave of his hand, the gateway opened for him, and he passed through back into his office. The mist spiraled where the gateway had been. The owl sat upon her perch, watching him with golden eyes. She knew more than she was letting on. But being his father's creature, she wouldn't tell him where to begin his search.

He might not know who was behind it, but he could guess who their next target was: Lady Thornton.

8

Catherine paced the length of her dressing room. The breeze, scented with wet earth and ash wood, did little to soothe the clawing anxiety that churned in her gut. She'd left her oaken door cracked open to remind herself that should she choose, she could walk through it at any time. It was something she could never have done in Elk Grove, where they bolted the doors at night, and the windows were nailed closed. Despite these measures, the dark wood paneling closed in upon her. Had she been given a choice, she would have dressed herself. It would have been quicker. Mrs. Morgan had remarked that the former Lady Thornton had been dressed by her lady's maid. If she were to remain here, she must adhere to all expectations, to not put a single toe out of line.

Not after she had fainted. Not after she had thought she'd seen the grisly murder of a woman, she had never met. Though she tried to put it from her mind, Miss Ashton's sightless blue eyes, the scent of blood, and the taste of bile in her mouth continued to linger. Her fits had been distressing

—ghosts of violent murders, creatures with pointed teeth, and sharp claws haunted her. But they felt pale and thin compared to this. Her throat clenched to think of it. Better to forget, to pretend it never happened. That was the only way forward. The alternative was to go back to Elk Grove and the ceaseless screaming, to Dr. Armstrong and the room.

The door creaked open, and footsteps approached. Catherine spun around wide-eyed, hands up to shield her from grasping hands. They'd come; they were going to send her back to Elk Grove.

"I'm sorry I kept you waiting, my lady," Miss Larson said, her brow quirked. A dress was slung over her arm.

Catherine lowered her hands to her side as her face flushed. If they didn't think her mad before, they would come to the conclusion soon enough. She had to control herself, hide her fear better. That was how she'd been able to convince Dr. Armstrong to release her. She'd fooled him; she could do it again.

"Thank you, and sorry to trouble you with fetching it for me. I'm not quite used to having others do this sort of thing for me," Catherine said, her voice shaking, but she held onto her smile. Was that the right thing to say? Perhaps it made her look too low? No matter what she did, she looked like a madwoman or a social ladder climber. Though she'd rather be the ladder climber if she must choose.

"No need. I dreamed of playing dress-up with a life-sized doll. It's much more fun than changing the sheets and stoking the fires." She winked.

Miss Larson draped the dress over the top of a privacy screen in the corner. Catherine followed after her as a prisoner does to execution. The thought of a stranger's hand touching her made her shoulders taut. In her darkest moments at Elk Grove, she had refused to eat; she wouldn't even rise to relieve herself. After a few days, the staff had roughly grabbed her, stripped her of her clothes, and tossed buckets of ice-cold water onto her. Over and over, she endured it until she resumed eating and using the chamber pot on her own. It was then as Dr. Armstrong had stood over her, telling her in his calm voice that he did it for her, to help her get well, that she had resolved to escape that horrid place. No matter what lies she must tell. No matter how many times she had to turn away and pretend not to see. Her body trembled as Miss Larson undid the buttons of her nightgown. She tried to push away the memories, but they buffeted against her like a storm. Her stomach roiled. Miss Larson wasn't one of those caretakers, but her body knew no way to distinguish the two. Even the barest brush of a finger against her back made her skin pimple.

"Is anything the matter, my lady? You're shivering like a leaf," Miss Larson said.

"I'm fine." She tried to keep her voice steady, but the fear still seeped out.

A moment's pause. A sharp inhalation of breath from behind her.

"If you'd prefer it, I can wait on the other side of the screen, hand you the garments, and button it once you're done." She said it very softly.

Catherine lowered her head. No one had offered her such a kindness before. No questions asked, no judgment. She was too ashamed to even raise her head and meet her gaze.

"Yes, thank you," Catherine said quietly.

Miss Larson backed away. Hidden by the screen, Catherine slid down the nightgown and let it pool on the ground at her feet. She reached for the day gown and slid it on, the fabric gliding over her skin like water. Once she was clothed again to the best of her ability, the shivering stopped. She stepped around the screen to where Miss Larson waited, eyes averted.

"Could you button me? I cannot reach," Catherine asked.

Miss Larson said not a word as she approached her slowly. "It will take just a moment," she said. Her warm breath brushed against the nape of Catherine's neck.

She rarely let anyone this close to her, but perhaps it was the delicate way in which she fashioned the buttons, or maybe because Catherine had invited her into her personal space, it did not scare her or make her tremble; instead, it felt not comfortable but not terrible either. It was a start, she supposed.

"Now that's done, would you like me to see to your hair?" Miss Larson asked.

Catherine always wore her hair rather simple in a braid and out of her face. And today, all she had planned was a carriage ride with Edward. Surely she shouldn't go to too much trouble. The wind would undo any work Miss Larson did anyway. "I don't want to be a bother."

"Not that it's any of my business..." she said and then stopped.

"But?" Catherine prompted; her throat felt tight.

"It's just I've overheard things Mrs. Oakheart has said about you..."

Catherine shrunk down in her seat. She didn't need to hear any more.

"Forgive me. I shouldn't have said that. It's just I am grateful to serve you. And you seem a kind woman." Her face flushed as she lowered her gaze. "This is why Mrs. Morgan wouldn't let me be a lady's maid and hired that girl from the city instead..."

Miss Larson's eyes glazed over, and she stared at the distance for a moment. It was the sort of look she'd seen among the residents of Elk Grove where the mind disconnected from the body. But this wasn't Elk Grove; those sorts of things didn't happen to regular people.

"Then how did you become my lady's maid?" Catherine prompted, hoping she was imaging this too.

Miss Larson shook herself and snapped her attention to Catherine. "What was that, my lady?"

She shouldn't press; she was already toeing that line too closely. But her gut told her to press on. Just in case... "You said Mrs. Morgan wouldn't let you be a lady's maid; there was someone else; did she work for Mrs. Oakheart?"

Miss Larson frowned. "I did?" She shook her head again. "Mrs. Oakheart was already married by the time I came to Thornwood...There was another girl...?" Her frown deepened, and she pressed her finger to her temple. "But, I cannot recall her clearly."

The ghost had warned Catherine she would be next. Both her and Miss Ashton had their hearts carved out. Could this forgotten maid be the ghost? Impossible. Improbable. Dangerous to even consider.

"Don't trouble yourself. It wasn't important." Catherine waved away the question as one would bat at a fly. "Why don't you advise me the best way to style my hair. Lord Thornton promised to take me out in his two-seater today."

"Oh splendid, I have just the idea." She clapped her hands together and got to work.

Catherine knocked on the double doors to Edward's study. Though they had an appointment, she still held her breath. An unintelligible reply that could have been "go away" or could have been "come in". She'd decided today she would be bold, and she eased the door open just enough to slide in. Edward sat at his desk, as he had the day before, his shirt unbuttoned and his cravat untied. The bags under his eyes were bigger than before, and it didn't appear he had changed clothes since yesterday. Had he not slept at all?

"Just set the tea things over there," he said and waved his hand toward the edge of his desk, where a tray with an untouched sandwich and teacup rested.

Catherine froze on the threshold. Edward must have forgotten about his promise. Maybe today wasn't a good day for a carriage ride. Of course, he was busy. Should she say something or slink away without a word?

"Umm. Edward?"

He glanced up. "Oh, Catherine. I wasn't expecting you...The carriage ride, darling, I am so sorry. I nearly forgot!"

He stood up and walked around the desk, approaching her in a few quick strides. In a blink, he was upon her and her shoulder blades collided with the wall as she backed away, unthinking.

She put up her hands, waving them in front of her. "No. I can see you're busy. Perhaps another time..." She inched toward the door.

"No, don't go." He grabbed her wrist. She tensed.

He let her go as if burned. Catherine exhaled, ashamed. He'd grabbed her so suddenly. She wanted to explain, but how could she admit the truth: that she lied to him in order to escape a worse fate?

She forced a smile, but it must have looked more like a grimace because Edward's brows pulled together tightly.

"I've been a terrible husband. After you fainted the other day, I should have been more concerned with your wellbeing than these damn wild dogs." He looked to the window where a rare stream of light peeked through. Then his gaze pinned her in place once more. "I've been meaning to take you on a tour of Thornwood since we arrived. The paperwork can wait, and I made you a promise after all."

Edward called for the two-seater, and while that was prepared, he went upstairs to change and wash. Catherine went outside to wait. The feel of warm sunshine on her face, and the scent of fresh grass eased the knot in her chest. She could do this; she would be the kind of wife worthy of Edward. She had to be.

※

THE DRIVER CAME AROUND WITH THE CARRIAGE MOMENTS before Edward emerged on the front steps looking refreshed and every inch the hero from a novel, as he had when they first met. Edward held out a hand for Catherine to take and helped her into the carriage. When she could see his hands, when she could brace for his touch, it was easy. She could almost pass for normal. The space in the carriage was snug, and they had no choice but to brush elbows. This was the first time they'd be mostly alone since their wedding day. She drew in her arms as close to her body as she could as her face flushed at the possibilities. Would he take them to some secluded spot and kiss her? Would he want more? She wasn't sure what to think.

"A bit cozy. I hope you don't mind." Edward gave her a smile, which she returned, but now her gut was twisting.

With a flick of his wrists, Edward got the carriage moving, and the dappled gelding tossed his mane, and they were on their way. They winded down country roads as Edward pointed out the different sights. He gestured to neighbors' homes: Mrs. Oakhearts, Mrs. Rosewoods, the local pub called The Fairy Bride, and the shops in the village square. Further out were farmhouses of tenant farmers, the reverend's cottage, the widow and her spinster daughter, and on and on, he filled the silence with chatter about Thornwood.

"These woods connect all the way to the back end of Thornwood Abbey," Edward remarked as they rode along them.

Eyes stared at her from the mist, and Catherine turned her head away. There was nothing there. It was just some woods. Nothing to fear from trees. She let his voice wash over her, and little by little, the tension in her shoulders relaxed. The scent of pine and mud, the kiss of the sun warming her skin, it was all so lovely. In novels, heroines went for enchanting tours with their lovers. She'd imagined what it would be like, but this was even better than what she could have imagined. She craned to get a look at the patches of wildflowers growing on the roadside. She'd never seen them before. She turned to ask Edward to stop for a moment and look at them. As she did, she saw his arm raised.

She flinched, anticipating a strike.

"I thought I would put my arm around you, but if you would prefer I didn't..." he asked.

She was spared from answering when an old woman stepped into the road and flagged them down. Edward had to pull hard on the reigns to avoid colliding with her. The gelding roared his displeasure as they came to a shuddering halt. Catherine lurched forward in her seat and grasped onto the front of the carriage to save herself from being flung forward and out.

"Lord Thornton! Thank goodness you are here. My husband, he's gotten trapped under his plow." The old woman came over, reaching for Edward with wrinkled hands.

He looked up to the sun up above, to Catherine, and then to the old woman. "Where is he?"

"In the south field, please hurry!" Her sagging face contorted with grief. "There was so much blood."

"Catherine, go with her, and I will go see what can be done. If he is injured, I would not want you to see it." His expression looked grim. What was he expecting to find? Accidents happened on farms; she'd heard enough stories. But Edward saw her as a delicate lady, not a woman who'd seen depraved things. She'd rather not shatter that illusion.

Edward took the time to help her out of the carriage. "Wait for me here. Do not go anywhere else, understand?" He fixed her with his gaze.

She nodded. Fear for the man and the unsettling, strange look in Edward's eyes made her uneasy. He glanced once more at the sky then to the forest before flicking the reigns and heading off in the direction of the field the old woman had indicated.

"Come, my lady. Come in for some tea." The old woman gestured up the road toward a cottage nestled against the forest. Clouds had rolled in and blotted out the sun. A shiver raced down Catherine's spine. Edward had been insistent she not leave this spot.

"I should wait for my husband," Catherine said.

Tears welled up in the woman's eyes. "Please, I fear for my William. It would bring me comfort if you joined me in my cottage for tea."

She couldn't say no. The woman must have been sick with worry. And it wasn't far, just a few feet away. She followed the old woman to her cottage. It had a thatched roof and worn, wood walls. Inside it was sparsely furnished with a double bed covered in a threadbare quilt and a wood table in the center worn smooth in places from years of use. A kettle over the fireplace whistled, and the old woman pulled it off the fire and filled two stone cups. The brew had a familiar scent, though she could not quite place it. Catherine wrinkled her nose.

"Oh. You should have something to eat. But my old legs aren't what they used to be. Would you go around the back into the woods fetch a bit of bread and cheese from my cellar?" she asked.

The hairs stood up on the back of Catherine's neck. The woman's words were a simple enough request. But those woods made her uneasy. The last time she'd gotten close to them, she'd seen that doorway. But how could she deny a distressed old woman?

"Yes, ma'am." Catherine stood up, and she thought from the corner of her eye the woman had changed. She looked younger, her skin a pale green. But when she looked again, she was the same old woman. Her head throbbed again, and the creeping feeling hadn't gone away. She shoved those thoughts aside. It must be a trick of the light.

A well-worn path led into the forest and, at the end, a mound with a door placed over it. That had to be the cellar she'd mentioned. Music drifted on the wind. It tugged at her with invisible hands. She inched closer, her ears buzzing with it. Caught at once in its spell, she could not turn away. The world around her seemed to bend and warp as she got closer. The leaves on the trees had a richer hue, the air smelt sweeter, and a prickle raced over her skin. Catherine shook her head and turned away from the forest. Something told her she shouldn't go here. Listening to these visions, these daydreams, was indulging them too much. She had to find the cellar and go back to the old woman and wait for Edward.

THE DOOR TO THE CELLAR WAS OPEN; SOMETHING PROPPED it up. As she inched closer, she found a wrinkled hand and nothing else attached to it but the bloody bone and sinew. She screamed and backed away.

A twig snapped behind her, and Catherine spun in place. The old woman strode toward her, head bowed.

"I scented the blood, but I did not know I would find fresh prey here."

She lifted her head, revealing black pupil-less eyes and sickly green skin and hair.

"What are you?" Catherine screamed.

The creature only smiled as she revealed pointed teeth. Catherine turned and ran into the forest.

9

The forest was unerringly still. Each labored breath echoed back at Ray as he stepped out from the shade of the trees and surveyed the dirt road. The wind rolled leaves end over end, and branches hanging over it swayed in the breeze. Not a sign of life in either direction. He strained his ears for the creak of carriage wheels, the beat of horse hooves, or even the crack of the whip. Silence answered. He'd really lost them around that last bend. By the Great Tree, now what?

Following Lady Thornton's carriage should have been easy. Among the trees, this close to the gateway between faery and the human realm, a glamour to disguise him in shadows and magic to make his footsteps swifter should have been effortless. If it were after the full moon, he might have used a tracking spell, or sent an ether messenger to follow her on his behalf. But he had precious little energy left before the full moon tonight. And he didn't have enough to keep up with them. His magic should have lasted longer, but lately, it seemed to run out faster and faster.

He turned back to the still forest. Fog gathered, swirling between sentinel ash and oak. Not a single bird called. No animal rustled in the brush. Odd.

Ray leaned against the rough bark of a nearby ash tree. This single road led in and out of Thornwood, wending past farmland and the forest, which encircled the village. If they'd gone this way, they'd have to come back this way. What was the use in exhausting himself when he might as well wait here?

A breeze rustled through the trees, and the hairs on the back of his neck stood on end. He felt eyes on him, but he kept his shoulders relaxed, only his finger twitched to reach for the dagger hidden at his hip. It might be another of Father's spies, come to watch him, make sure he wasn't killing more girls. The wind changed directions. His nostrils flared. It was faint, but he smelled blood. Perhaps waiting around was the wrong strategy.

He ran along the road until he came upon a farmhouse set back from the road. Just as still and silent as the forest. Normally one would expect to hear animals, chickens, or penned animals. But he heard nothing at all. Just the faint creak of an open door in the wind. He grasped the hilt of his dagger and approached the cottage.

He eased open the door, ears pricked for the killer. Overturned tables blocked the entrance, and blood smeared the walls. The stench turned his stomach, but unlike the woman he'd found on the side of the road, there was no stench of arcane magic. Just a musky scent he couldn't quite place.

He squeezed past the table and entered the room. No body. But a spilled pot, half-cooked carrots, and potatoes strewn onto the floor, chunks of rotting meat in gray broth. He wrinkled his nose. Not Lady Thornton then, and whoever had done this, was long gone. Not his problem. He sheathed his dagger and headed for the door.

A pool of congealed blood on the floor had tracks leading away from it. Animal prints. A wolf? But wolves had been gone from this area for centuries. He squatted down, much too big to be a wolf anyway. Ray's eyes widened. Not wolf prints, they were much larger than any wolf. A werewolf. First, the blood magic and now werewolves?

They weren't unheard of outside of Faery, but usually, they only crossed over during the full moon. At times when their bite didn't kill, they turned their victims. That meant there was an infected hunting the farms. He ran out of the cottage, dagger drawn as he followed the trail of blood-flecked feathers. It had left a trail of paw prints in the soft earth, and he followed it past the pigpen where the partially devoured carcasses of pigs had begun to rot.

The tracks disappeared into the forest. Finding Lady Thornton would have to wait. Unless tamed, a werewolf would be a devouring force, and left unchecked, it would turn more humans until they were either dead or slathering blood-thirsty monsters. He followed the trail through the mist to where it abruptly ended in the middle of the forest. Ray turned slowly, dagger held out in front of him.

It wasn't unusual for a werewolf in the human realm to abruptly transition. He would have expected to find an indent on the ground where the body had lain, or broken branches and trampled undergrowth where he had contorted with the transformation. From there, he would have expected to see a man's footsteps leading away. But he saw no such thing. The footsteps stopped along a creek. The prints nearly washed away. It ambled through the forest in both directions and eventually met up with a river. They could follow it for miles, double back, or create false trails. Farmers watered their animals at this creek, women washed their clothes. He'd never find the wolf this way.

This wasn't some unfortunate soul consumed by a curse. They were intelligent enough in wolf form to know to cover up their tracks. And that made this even more dangerous. Ray sighed and raked his hands through his hair. He didn't sign up for this. Even if he found the killer in time, now he had to contend with werewolves?

That decided it; he was leaving Thornwood. Father couldn't punish him if he couldn't find him. He'd get on a ship, head for the east of the human realm. Even Father could not access the gateways there. He should have done it decades ago.

Ray turned on his heel, eyes fixed on the horizon. In his pocket were a few human coins. Hopefully, they were enough to get him where he wanted to go. If not, he was strong enough to menial work to earn his way. Ray stood frozen in place, hand on the hilt of his dagger. The eyes were still watching him. He could feel it. Despite his resolution, he couldn't make his feet move. Leaving Thornwood meant never coming back; those were the rules of his exile. Should he try to escape that way, the Thorn Kingdom would forever be barred to him.

What's the use? If Father would never let him return, why keep pretending? Ray clenched his hand into a fist and inhaled.

An owl screeched, and he twisted his head as it circled overhead.

"Lady Thornton, she is in danger. You must come straight away!" she cried.

She flew into the forest, and Ray didn't hesitate to follow after her.

CATHERINE'S FEET SLIPPED IN DECOMPOSING LEAVES. She threw out her arm and clawed the bark of a tree to keep her balance. Each breath burned. Her legs ached. Fog enshrouded the forest; the landscape all looked the same. Had she run past that tree already? Where was the road? Should she cry out and hope Edward was close enough to hear? What about another farmhouse where she could beg for shelter? Twigs snapped, the sound like the crack of brittle bones. Don't stop. She gathered up the hem of her skirt and kept running.

"Run all you like; it only makes the meat sweeter." The creature's mocking voice came from in front of her, so Catherine veered to the right.

The cackle of its laughter surrounded her. It seemed to be coming from all directions. Catherine weaved in and out of trees, praying that would lose it. But what if she didn't. Could she fight it off? When she was a girl, the small folk who visited her garden had been terrified of an iron spade. They told her iron hurt them. What she wouldn't give for a nail or a piece of mere scrap iron. But that would mean it was all real. This could just be another hallucination. It couldn't hurt her if it weren't real.

Fear tingled across her skin, and she flushed with heat as her heart raced. Despite every part of her screaming to keep running, she skidded to a stop and turned. Catherine couldn't keep running from shadows. Dr. Armstrong told her she had to face her fears. She balled her hands into fists. She couldn't see much beyond the reach of her hand. Not real. Not real. Catherine screwed her eyes and counted down from ten. Nine. Eight. Seven.

Laughter slithered into her ear. "Done running, are you? What fun is that?"

Six. Five. Four.

A hand wrapped around her from behind, nails clawing across her neck. Her hairs stood on end, and the flesh on her arm pebbled. Not real. She swallowed past a lump in her throat.

"Two. One." She finished aloud. Her voice echoed back at her in the stillness and silence of the forest.

Hot, rancid breath brushed against her cheek. "Your spell won't save you, girl."

Her insides turned to water. She couldn't move. Run. Run. RUN! Her mind screamed, but her arms were pinned to her side, her feet weighed down by invisible stones. The hand clenched her throat, and she gasped for a wheezing breath.

"I smelled you from leagues away, fae child. I never thought you would be this easy to lure away. But humans can be compassionate fools, can't they?"

The edges of her vision turned black. Tears pressed at the back of her lids, but she refused to let them fall. The screech of an owl cut through the air. The creature hissed, and the pressure around her neck slackened. Catherine's hand shot to her throat, and she pressed her tender flesh.

"Lady Thornton?" She blinked. Mr. Thorn stepped through the mist.

Had it been a hallucination? In her insanity, had she wandered into the forest? Chased by her own insanity.

"Are you real?" she croaked. Her throat ached.

He stopped, and his brows shot up to his hairline. "The last I checked, I was." He patted a long-fingered hand against his shirt.

She cracked a smile, though it felt inappropriate to do so. She felt as if she were unraveling like a spool of thread. And she was reaching the end. Hysteria clawed at her insides, twisted her stomach into knots. Either a monster had attacked her and nearly choked life out of her, or her madness was getting worse. She wasn't sure which was a more troubling prospect.

"How did you get here, are you hurt?" He approached her, hand out as one would a wild animal or a rabid dog.

"I don't—" The words caught in her throat.

The thing crept up behind him, her green, mottled skin sloughed off in chunks. Thin strands of dark hair clung to her bulbous head. It couldn't be real, and yet it was drawing closer to Mr. Thorn. Its dagger-like teeth were dripping with bright green saliva.

Mr. Thorn canted his head to the side. "You don't?"

"Look out!" She gasped at the same moment the creature lunged.

It latched onto him from behind. Long, clawed fingers dug into his shoulders, and thin spindly legs wrapped around his waist. He twisted in its grip as it clamped dagger-like teeth into the meat of his arm. Mr. Thorn groaned and ran backward, slamming the creature into a nearby tree.

It seemed to have stunned her because, for a moment, the creature unhooked her legs, and they dangled as Mr. Thorn wrestled to pull her latched bite off his arm. Thick green ooze poured from the wound, and Mr. Thorn's steps turned sluggish. He swayed on his feet. The creature had a venomous bite.

An owl screeched, and Catherine flinched as it flew just past her head and landed at the base of a nearby tree. It used its wing to gesture toward a rock half-buried in leaf debris and soft earth. Did it want her to take up the rock and strike the creature with it? But owls couldn't communicate like that. This entire thing was madness. If she closed her eyes and counted down would this all go away?

Mr. Thorn stumbled and fell onto one knee. He climbed up again and staggered backward again, trying to slam the creature into a tree a second time. Real or not, she had to do something. Catherine clawed at the earth and pulled at the rock until it broke free. She had to use both hands to lift it as dirt fell in clumps from it.

They had their backs to her as she crept up behind them; her arms shook with the effort as she lifted the stone above her head and brought it down hard on the creature's skull. A crunch and a scream, it turned toward her, lips coated in blood. It hissed as it leaped toward her.

"You'll regret this," she hissed. Catherine threw her arms up to shield herself, eyes screwed shut.

Something hit the ground with a thump. Catherine waited for the blow that never came. She cracked one eye open. Mr. Thorn knelt over the limp body of the creature. A pool of greenish blood pooled on the leaves and soaked the earth. Catherine's shaking knees collapsed beneath her. The creature's sightless eyes stared up at her, teeth open with malice, and the gash in its skull wept green blood.

"Are you hurt?" Mr. Thorn asked, though his voice sounded like it was underwater.

Catherine blinked up at him.

This couldn't be real. She must be dreaming. But her throat ached where the creature had tried to strangle her, and the sharp, acidic scent of its blood turned her stomach. Her nails were caked with dirt from digging out the rock. Mr. Thorn grimaced and reached for the place where the creature had bitten him. Blood trickled from the tear in his clothes, and the skin beneath was ragged and torn.

"You're hurt. We should call for a doctor." She tried to climb to her feet, but her legs shook and threatened to give way beneath her.

"I'm fine, but you look ready to collapse. Lean upon me if you need to." He held out his good arm for her to steady herself upon.

He did not move to grasp her or hold her against her will. It was a small gesture, but one she was startled to realize she'd never been given before. It was up to her to lean upon him if she so wished. Hesitatingly, she grasped his forearm. It felt as steady as an ancient oak branch.

"I must say, keeping you safe is a full-time job," Mr. Thorn mused as they started walking back through the misty forest.

"What do you mean?" The words escaped her in a rush.

"The last time we met, there was a body." He said it as casually as one mentions the weather.

Catherine stopped in her steps. She swallowed past a lump in her throat. She couldn't have heard that right. She'd imagined Miss Ashton's murder...

"I don't know what you're talking about." She shook her head, and tried to keep her voice even. Perhaps this was a trick. He wanted to catch her, expose her for her madness.

Or was it madness? His arm was still bleeding, and he wobbled slightly. An ashen pallor had taken over his skin. Was she imagining that as well? No. Better to pretend. To look the other way was always easier.

"You don't know, or you don't want to admit it?" He shook his head and pressed a palm to his temple.

No one ever questioned her. From Mama and Papa, to the caretakers at Elk Grove, they were all quick to smooth things over. Willing to deny all the signs until they became inconvenient, until Catherine disobeyed.

"Why is it that humans continue to deny what is staring them in the face?" He slurred his words as he leaned onto a nearby tree. He braced himself and stared at the ground.

She locked her eyes on the ground. Her heart pounded in her throat. If this were real. If all of it was the truth... the creature, the murders, everything, what did that mean...years of torment...all of it for nothing?

"Because I'm afraid." The words slid out of her barely above a whisper.

She wasn't sure why she'd said it aloud. Perhaps it was shock, or maybe it was resignation. If she were truly descending into madness, there was no way to hide it any longer.

"There's nothing wrong with being afraid, Lady Thornton." Her gaze shot up.

All her life, she'd been taught to ignore what was inconvenient, so she'd hidden behind a mask. His eyes were fever bright, and he seemed to only be standing by sheer force of will. Then he pitched forward, collapsing onto one knee. She took a step forward, then held herself back. What should she do? He needed help, but as she scanned the forest around them, she wasn't entirely sure which way she needed to go to get back to the village or the manor.

His breathing was heavy and labored. She approached him warily. If it were all the truth, then the ghost with her carved up body was real, and Mr. Thorn was her killer. If all this were real... she might be in danger. Catherine stood back, hands twisted together. A light sheen of sweat dotted his brow. If he were a murderer, why had he saved her from that creature?

At the very least, she should find help; the rest she would have to figure out later. One step at a time, first to get him aid. She held out a hand. He stared up at her, his hair falling into his eyes.

"What's this then?" he asked, the faintest hint of a smile on his face.

Catherine jutted her hand out again. "I'll help you back to the road. My husband can't be very far. We'll take you back to Thornwood," she said with more conviction than she felt.

He studied her outstretched appendage for a moment before he grasped it. The feel of his palm against hers was warm and alive. She tensed, but the moment was brief. She'd braced herself for his touch. She took a deep breath and guided his arm around her shoulder. A wave of anxiety crashed over her causing her to think of that strong arm encircling her, crushing her windpipe, grasping her, and dragging her to the room. She exhaled a ragged breath. His arm hung limply around her shoulder, and he did not rest his palm against her, though it would have made balancing easier for him. He kept his arm bent just so as to not touch her more than necessary. No one had been that considerate of her comfort before.

"Human remedies are useless against an Oshrin bite. There will be an antidote in Faery," he said.

She broke out in a cold sweat. She must have misheard him. Faery was the place the small folk had begged her to go.

That was where they said they came from. The same place she'd been running from since then.

"What?"

He gestured toward the right. The faint notes of a song tugged at her, and the sensation of a current pulled at her legs. But she still dared not look.

"Hnng." Mr. Thorn sucked in air sharply.

There was no time for second-guessing. She couldn't risk a man's life while she questioned her own sanity. She looked up, and the same vine-covered gateway she'd seen in the garden at Thornwood greeted her. She took a faltering step toward it, and as she approached, the vines rolled back and opened onto a moonlit forest. Faery. The word whispered through her mind. Her skin prickled, and her heart raced. This was madness surely. But the pull was undeniable now, the ache so painful she feared it would rend her apart.

"Not to rush you, but if the venom reaches my heart, I will die. If you do not wish to enter, I will not force you."

Catherine swallowed down her fear. "No, I will take you." And together, they stepped through the gateway.

10

One step before the other. Catherine passed through the gateway, and a slight tingle touched her skin. A chill wind blew, and she trembled. In the moonlight, the trees had a faint blue sheen, their leaves silvery with dark purple veins. Thick grass grew in clumps at the base of the trees, the green so vibrant it glowed faintly. Catherine drank it all in wide-eyed. It felt as if she had stumbled into a dream world.

"We need to just follow this path," Mr. Thorn said with a groan. His arm trembled as he balanced on her shoulder.

Flowering bushes hip-high grew along the narrow path. She followed it, and as her skirts brushed against the brush, tight pink buds bloomed, releasing a tantalizingly sweet scent. It reminded her of honey cakes and buttery caramels she'd loved as a child. If this were a dream, it was the most vivid one she'd ever had. She glanced over her shoulder back to the gateway, but it had disappeared. She snapped her head forward. Don't think about it. Keep moving. Get Mr. Thorn to safety.

Her throat still ached, and now a lump had lodged itself there. She could only manage a nod in reply. Where were they going? His home? Did he live in this strange forest as the small folk who'd visited her as a child had? What did that make him? Her heart stuttered in her chest to think of it.

Glowing eyes blinked at her from the shadows. The too-bright grass rustled as they passed. High pitched voices chattered to one another in the treetops, shaking branches and raining leaves down on their heads. Catherine kept her eyes forward.

"Ignore them; they smell the human realm on you. But they are harmless," Mr. Thorn said.

Catherine swiveled her head toward Mr. Thorn, mouth slack. It was still a surprise to hear him acknowledge the small folk. No one ever seemed to see them but her. In her surprise, she miscalculated how close they were together. With his arm around her shoulder, his face was inches from hers. Sweat plastered his brow, and green ooze streaked his hair to his forehead. His dark eyes transfixed her; she could see her own reflection in them. His cheekbones were sharp and the hollows of his cheeks a little more sunken, but combined with his dark eyes and full soft lips, his beauty was both dazzling and terrifying. Was this his true face, the one the fae hid away? She blushed and turned away. This was inappropriate, or perhaps the more accurate term was this was ludicrous. The fae weren't real. And yet here she was helping one who was deathly injured to places unknown.

Something brushed past her ankle, and she leaped back, causing her side to graze Mr. Thorn's accidentally. He pressed his hand lightly on her waist, and she stiffened. Panic jolted through her. This was it, the moment he'd turn against her and harm her. As quickly as he'd brushed against her, he pulled back. Taking his arm from around her shoulders, he stumbled and braced himself upon a nearby tree with long, tan fingers.

"Forgive me, I didn't mean to frighten you. I can walk on my own from here; it's not much further," he said as trembles racked his body.

Mr. Thorn pushed off the tree, shoulders taut as he clutched his bleeding arm and ambled down the path. She followed after him. She had not much choice otherwise. She wasn't sure she knew where to go or how to find home. It felt as if she were floating, or better yet drifting down a river, and the current was moving faster and faster, her head dipping underwater, and no matter how hard she tried to stay at the surface, she would be pulled under. Her chest felt tight. She was in Faery with one of the fae. Catherine balled her hand into a fist at her side to hide its trembling. She could hardly comprehend the reality of her situation, let alone voice it aloud.

As they walked, the song she'd heard outside of the gateway drifted over her. It felt as if it were all around them. Before, she'd mistaken it for a single singer, but now she could hear the individual voices as they wove together into one. It filled her with a sensation that was both joyful and mournful. Though she couldn't understand the words, she felt as if they were telling her a story, one both familiar and foreign.

She looked around the forest, seeking out the singer. They were alone but for the trees... it couldn't be coming from the trees? For as long as she could remember, she felt a certain connection to plants and all things that grew. At times it felt like they were speaking to her without words. She knew when they needed more sunlight or more water. If the soil were too wet or missing a certain nutrient. At Elk Grove, they'd called it a knack for growing. But secretly, she'd kept inside how they whispered to her without words. She feared if she confessed that they would take away even the garden from her. She inched closer to the trees, her hand outstretched to press against their smooth trunks. They were faintly warm and thumped a pulse like a slow heartbeat. It sent a small thrill through her.

"You can hear it, can't you?" Mr. Thorn said. He frowned slightly.

Catherine yanked her hand away and turned toward him. She'd lost herself for a moment in the song. Even now, it pulsed against her, a hunger that threatened to consume her. He saw the small folk; did he hear their singing as well? But if he did... if he did...

The mournful cry of a wolf cut the forest's song short. A yawning silence followed in the absence of the tree song. Mr. Thorn's wide-eyed gaze swept over the forest surrounding them.

"Come, there isn't much time." He gestured for her to follow, and he quickened his pace.

She didn't question the urgency in his voice and kept close to him as they followed a trail through the trees. It ended at an oak that was three times the width of her arm span and whose canopy stretched far above the treetops and disappeared against the dark night sky. The roots grew up to her shoulders, and thick blankets of moss coated them. A divot between them led to a wooden door that disappeared into the bark of the tree.

Mr. Thorn shuffled closer and pressed his face nearly to the wood and whispered something against the bark. It was lost as the sound of the wolf howl had gotten closer. The hairs on the back of her neck stood on end. Edward had mentioned wild dogs killing the livestock of his tenant farmers. What if they hadn't been wild dogs at all but something much more deadly? She scanned the forest, expecting a slathering monster to leap out at her at any moment. A brush of warm air hit her back, and she turned to see the door open onto the golden light of a room beyond.

"Inside, before it finds us." Mr. Thorn gestured for her to step in first. His eyes were on the full moon overhead. She ducked to step into the hollow of the tree.

The interior was deceptively large. A corridor with a carpet of bright green moss led onto an open living area and further down another wall. Lights hung from fibers in the ceiling and flickered a strange bluish-green. A single cot pressed against the wall was covered in a blanket that looked sewn together with bits of discarded fabric. Blue and red feathers poked out from within a hole in one of the patchwork seams. A cauldron hung on a hook over the cold fireplace, a pile of wood and kindling sat next to, as if the house's owner had stepped out and would soon return to light the hearth. Mr. Thorn stumbled over to the cot and collapsed upon it. Feathers fluttered up, and an old musty smell filled her nostrils.

Sitting on the edge of the bed, Mr. Thorn tore off his sleeve and exposed the corded muscles of his arm. A bloody gash where the creature had bitten him bled, and from it, black veins traveled up and over his shoulder and under his shirt. Catherine turned away. It was inappropriate to stare. A blush burned the back of her neck. Of all the things she'd seen today, a man's bare arm was what she was worried about? But he wasn't really a man, was he? Catherine shook her head.

The musk of dried herbs drifted on the cool, damp air. The wall opposite the bed was lined with shelves hewn from the earth. Roots wove in and out of the wall and created hooks and lines from which herbs were dried. They were crammed full of strange odds and ends like water-logged plants, dried roots of indeterminate origin, what looked suspiciously like lizard tails floating in purple goo, and crystals that caught the blue-green light and sparkled faintly.

"Would you mind bringing me that opaque jar on the middle shelf with the green liquid?" Mr. Thorn asked. His voice sounded strained, as if he were holding back immense pain.

Having a task to focus on, she jumped to do as he asked. Her hand hovered over the assortment of jars, some with strange herbs floating inside and others with things that looked suspiciously like eyeballs. She swallowed past the lump in her throat. Better not to wonder what it was all for. The bottle he'd indicated sat between two others of mystery liquid: one a dark red like blood with floating flakes of gold, and the other an inky black with what looked to be a white snake coiled inside. She snatched up the jar he'd indicated and scurried from the shelf to hand it over. He popped off the cork with his thumb and took a swig of the contents, draining it in one gulp. With a grimace, he set the empty jar on the nightstand beside the bed.

"Great Tree, that is awful." He leaned back, and his Adam's apple bobbed as he took in deep breaths.

The top buttons of his shirt pulled, and the tanned planes of his chest peeked out from beneath. His breathing was returning to normal. But her reality wasn't. The room remained the same—filled with strange curios. The man across from her had been bitten by the same creature that chased her. He himself was fae. Questions, doubts, and fears were rushing in like a river whose dam broke. Why was it whenever something strange happened he was there? Why had he endured such pain to protect her? They'd only shared a handful of words. In her favorite novel, Lady of the Moors, the hero Tristan took a shot for Angelique. But heroes weren't accused murderers, and heroines weren't mad women.

The very thought made her head spin. But was she mad? She fanned out her nails covered in grime from digging out the dirt. This place felt all too real. Too real. If she weren't insane, then her treatment, those years enduring Dr. Armstrong's cruel remedies, it was for nothing? Even more troubling if she weren't mad, that meant Mr. Thorn was a killer.

Her eyes darted back to Mr. Thorn. They were locked alone here, and she had no clue as to where she was. She needed to get out of here. Back home to Thornwood, where everything made sense... She glanced back to the door. If she followed that path, would it eventually lead to the edge of the forest, could she follow it to the road and back home?

"Thinking of running away already?" Mr. Thorn said, cracking one eye and piercing her with it.

Her pulse jumped. "If you're better, I should be getting back home..."

He sat up straight, elbows resting on his knees, and studied her a moment. "You're not what I expected. Normally humans ask more questions about this." He gestured around the room.

She wrapped her arms around her chest and resisted the urge to look around. She'd be lying to say she wasn't curious. But this felt wrong and forbidden. What would Dr.

Armstrong say? If she told him about any of this, he would have locked her in the room for a week or more. She shouldn't be here. She lowered her gaze to the floor.

"If you would tell me the way, I will leave you be." Her voice shook.

He heaved a sigh. The bed creaked as he stood and every heavy footfall as he crept closer to her felt as if echoed inside her. The ghost's warning rang in her ears. *You'll be next.* What a fool she'd been to trust him. She dug her nails into her arm until it ached. She backed up a step and collided with a chair. It tipped over with a clatter. She turned to run, but he was standing in her way.

"Stay back," she shouted. She couldn't breathe; her chest felt tight. Miss Ashton's sightless eyes, her bloody clothes. The ghost with her carved-up chest. Mr. Thorn connected to both. How could she have trusted him for even a moment?

He held up his hands to show her no harm. There was a dagger at his hip that she hadn't noticed before. Was that what he'd used to kill the others? "I know it can be overwhelming at first..." he said.

"The ghost, she warned me about you. Please, I saved your life, don't take my heart." Catherine's voice wavered. She clutched the fabric over her own heart, and her eyes darted toward his weapon. If she were very quick, she might take it from him and then and then...

"You saved my life, Lady Thornton. To the fae, that is a debt that must be repaid. Until it is, I cannot possibly harm a hair on your head."

It might be a trick. It might not. She wasn't sure what was real anymore. Before she could second-guess herself, she lurched forward and grasped for the dagger. Her fingertips brushed against the hilt before he had his hands around her wrist and pulled her backward.

She stood back, chest heaving. She'd been too slow. Perhaps a bit reckless too. There wouldn't be a second chance now. She looked around, searching for an escape.

He watched her with a smirk playing on his lips. "I must admit, I wasn't expecting that from you, Lady Thornton."

He drew his dagger from the hilt. Catherine wriggled free of his grasp and backed up until her back hit the cold earthen wall. Her eyes widened as he raised the dagger until it was inches from her throat. She clenched her eyes shut. This was it, the end to her miserable life.

Seconds passed, and the blade didn't pierce her skin. She peaked an eye open to see the dagger hovering over her skin, blocked by an invisible barrier. Mr. Thorn's face contorted with effort. He hadn't lied; he really couldn't hurt her.

He took several steps back and then held out the dagger to her hilt first. "Take it if it will make you more comfortable."

He watched her, dark eyes gleaming with amusement. She eyed him for a moment, wondering if this, too, were a trick. She reached for the dagger slowly. The hilt was warm from his grip, and the weight of it felt strange in her hand. But it was a comforting weight. She'd never been given the means to protect herself before. When she had a firm hold of it, he stepped back again.

"There we are. And while we're on the subject, I didn't kill those girls."

If he hadn't, who had? Her shoulders slumped. Had she accused her savior without cause? On the word of a ghost... To even consider believing a ghost's word felt absurd...

"Why did that—" She couldn't say the words aloud. As

bizarre as this all was, she still couldn't bring herself to acknowledge the madness of it all.

"Why did the ghost think I did it? Well, I intend to find out." His jaw was set, and it forbid any further inquiry. "Enough about me; I believe you said you wanted to get back home?" he said, the smile back on his face.

A howl echoed through the night, and Catherine's head jerked in that direction. She'd heard it in the forest, but it sounded much closer than that.

"I was afraid of that," Mr. Thorn said with a frown.

"Afraid of what?"

"The werewolf followed us here. We'll have to take an alternate route to get you home, unless you would rather try and outrun an intelligent and bloodthirsty predator?"

Her stomach flopped at the thought. "No."

"Didn't think so. But there is one thing; we will have to travel through Faery to get you home, and unless you want to remain here forever, you'll have to trust me." He held out his hand for her to take.

Catherine chewed on her bottom lip and picked at the skin on her nails. She wasn't sure. She'd come this far, but if she went deeper, she wasn't sure what she would discover. The wolf howled again, and she jumped in surprise. It was between a monster at the door or Mr. Thorn. Did she have any choice at all?

"I trust you."

11

The wolf howled, and the door rattled. Earth rained down on their heads from the ceiling. Mr. Thorn placed himself between Catherine and the door, reaching for the dagger, which was no longer at his hip. His eyes scanned the room as the wolf scratched and huffed on the other side of the door. Catherine's slick palms clutched the dagger Mr. Thorn had given her.

"Why did it follow us?" Ray muttered under his breath as he watched the door, which shook from another blow by the wolf.

She felt as if she were in a dream, or more like a nightmare, one from which she couldn't wake.

"Go to the door at the end of the hall. It is our safest way out." He nodded toward the door she'd noticed when they'd first come in.

She ran for it, wanting to put as much space as possible between her and the wolf. The doorknob was made of smooth polished wood, and roots weaved in and out through the gaps in the door. Catherine grasped it with sweaty palms, and the door opened with a whoosh of damp air and onto a long dark stairwell leading down underground into absolute darkness. She took a step back. The distant wail of patients filled her ears, and she felt rough hands on her shoulders. Catherine put her hands over her ears to block out the sound. She couldn't go into the room. She'd been bad to believe any of this was real. She'd behave. She'd promised she'd behave.

She backed into something soft and firm. Dr. Armstrong would force her inside. She whirled around and found not the physician but Mr. Thorn regarding her with a furrowed brow. The door creaked as wood cracked. Her eyes darted over his shoulder just as the wolf's black and gray muzzle poked through. It snuffled before retreating and growling. Its claws tearing at bits of wood. It would be through in a few minutes.

"We'll be safe in the tunnels. We can lose him there," Mr. Thorn said.

Catherine clasped her throat and shook her head. She couldn't. Not into the enclosed dark. "I can't," she whimpered.

Mr. Thorn looked from the stairwell to the door, where a paw tipped in yellowed claws pulled at a board that groaned, about to break. He held up his hand, and in his palm, a small green flame flickered.

"We won't be in the underground long. If you want, I can hold your hand." He held out his hand to her.

Her breathing eased slightly. The flame was small, but it gave off faint glowing warmth. Between that and dagger in her grip, she felt reassured. She would go into darkness, but it wouldn't be alone. With her free hand, she grasped his, and his larger hand enveloped her. The warmth felt like an anchor. The wave of panic hadn't ebbed completely, but it was manageable at least.

Mr. Thorn led the way down the stairs, and once they were inside, he slammed the door shut behind them. They were plunged into darkness but for the faint green light of his flame, which cast strange shadows across his face. Her heart clenched, and she froze in place. Panic crept back up again, clawing at her insides, twisting her apart. The complete darkness reminded her of feeling her heart thundering in her chest as she pleaded and pleaded to be let go until she would cry herself into exhaustion.

"You're safe. I've got you," he said.

His words soothed her, and little by little, they inched down the steps. Her legs trembled, but she kept moving forward. The luminous green glow led their way and the sound of the wolf's howls faded. They reached the bottom of the stairs into a space where their footsteps echoed back at them. Mr. Thorn held the light above them, and it grew a little brighter though his arm trembled to hold it up.

Three corridors, equally dark and cavernous. A moment's deliberation, and he chose the pathway to the right. They did this several more times; the pitch-black labyrinth seemed unending. How he knew which turns to make among the many was beyond her. He strode with the confidence of someone who'd done this a thousand times.

After what felt to be an eternity stumbling in the dark, she felt bold enough to ask, "Where are we going?"

"I need to replenish my magic in one of the small courts. I suspect that wolf didn't find us by accident. It seems to be hunting something." His expression was difficult to read in the half-dark, but his tone made her stomach twist. "To open the gateway back to the human realm, I'll need to replenish my magic. Even these small efforts are draining me." He sighed and held up the faintly flickering flame. It had begun to fade and gave off barely enough light to illuminate his hand.

If he were to be believed, someone had framed him for murder, and now they'd sent a killer after him. What had he done to create such enemies? She kept this to herself because she was terrified of the answer. The path began to slope upward, and the dark eased as moonlight illuminated their exit. They stepped out into the clean, crisp air which smelled of pine and wet earth after the rain. The air vibrated with the unspoken, and it sent a pleasant chill down her spine. The tree's song was clearer here, and the ache it created in her became even more painful.

"How do you replenish your magic?" Her voice felt distant, as if it belonged to a stranger.

"We dance together. The communion of the fae beneath the full moon shares the energy which flows from the Great Tree and brings life to all of Faery and the realms beyond..."

His voice faded away, and her gaze was transfixed by golden lights bobbing against the blue-black silhouette of trees and beyond that, a flickering flame of a bonfire. Shadows moved around, their shapes contorting and bending along the trees. It was there that the song led her. It called to her, urging her to join in the dance. That strange feeling of joy and sorrow swelled in her chest once more, and she wanted to laugh, to weep, to dance barefoot beneath the moonlight. Water lapped at her boots as she stood at the water's edge. She hadn't even realized she'd drawn closer.

"Careful, Lady Thornton. Lose yourself in the music, and

there is no escape. You'll become one with the rocks and trees."

"Wouldn't that be lovely? To be a tree, to feel no pain, to be rooted in a place unmovable for all time," she said in a dreamy way. She could already imagine it: her feet burying in the earth, spreading outward into a web of roots, her hands raised up to greet the sky, and leaves upturned drinking in the sunlight.

Mr. Thorn covered both her ears with his hands, and she came back to reality. Her vision filled by his handsome face. Her head buzzed as if she'd had too much to drink and too little to eat. She should have been afraid of having him this close, being uncertain of his intentions. But the song had seeped into her bones, had woven itself with the fiber of her being. She feared nothing with the music filling her ears. All her worries felt distant, as if they belonged to another person or were only a half-remembered dream after waking.

"As we are here, you will drink not of the faery cup nor eat from their table."

His words rushed over her from the top of her head to the tips of her toes, and she tingled as if she'd been dunked in cold water. Without intending to, she found herself nodding along. He let go of her ears and smiled, but his face was ashen, and the hollows of his cheeks more sunken than before. She'd seen that sickly look on patients at Elk Grove after long stints in the room without water, sunlight, food, or sleep. A human pushed to their absolute limits. He had said he needed to replenish his magic. Had he used up what little he had left to stop the song's effect on her?

"The small courts celebrate the Thorn Moon each month, and many bring humans for their entertainment, so you won't look too out of place. But you must stay close to me. They will do their best to try and ensorcell you."

Her head ached. Small court? Dances and Thorn Moons? She shook her head again. Mr. Thorn alighted onto a mossy rock in the creek. A row of them acted as a bridge across to the other side. He held a hand out to her once again. The creek burbled as she teetered there. Could she do this? The song called to her, although more distant than before.

"Lady Thornton?" Mr. Thorn asked.

Surely this was madness. And yet nothing had ever felt more right. The tips of her fingers brushed against Mr. Thorn's, and he pulled her onto the slick, mossy rocks. She wobbled on unsteady feet, the hand clutching the dagger held out for balance. Mr. Thorn grasped her by her waist and pulled her flush against his chest. Her heart thundered against the steady rhythm of his, and their eyes met. For the first time, she didn't fear the touch of another. He could not hurt her. Mr. Thorn looked away and cleared his throat. He hopped onto the next rock and helped her leap to the next, keeping his eyes averted. It was so utterly absurd that laughter bubbled out of her. To think the man she'd believed a killer would give her comfort in this strange place.

Mr. Thorn turned back to smile in reply. It made him even more charming. On the opposite bank, her shoes sank into the mud and dirtied the hem of her skirt. She didn't care; she'd never felt more alive.

Faces watched them from the trees. Not the same glowing eyes from before. But the trees themselves. Elegant women, hair coiffed, and the color of green leaves, the folds of their gowns made out of bark. Catherine stared at them in wide-eyed wonder.

"You heard their songs before. What did you think?" Mr. Thorn asked her.

"Beautiful," Catherine said in an awed whisper.

They shook their branches, and their song swelled around her as gentle as floating upon a bed with the softest down covers.

Mr. Thorn laughed, and it was husky and pleasant. "I think they are pleased."

A girl with a small sharp nose, round black eyes, and an owl mask pushed back on her head, darted past them, and stooped for a moment at a small pool of water. She dipped her long fingers into the water, splashed it on her face, and dunked in her bird feet. Catherine did a double take. She must have audibly gasped because the girl turned to look at her with golden owl-like eyes and tilted her head to one side as she observed her. The owl child scurried away as they approached the pool. She headed toward the bonfire where the dancing happened. Mr. Thorn didn't expect her to dance, did he? She was never skilled at dancing.

"Before we see the queen, we must wash," Mr. Thorn leaned in to whisper in her ear, and her skin prickled with his close proximity.

"Queen?" she gasped and looked down at her muddy boots and dirty hem. She was in no state to meet a queen, fae, or otherwise.

He chuckled again. "Don't worry, the spring washes all away." He gestured toward the pool.

Water sprung up from an unseen source in the pool, and the lip was lined with smooth river stones. After tucking the dagger into her bodice, she dipped her hands into cool crisp water and splashed her face. Mr. Thorn shed his boots and washed his feet, then looked to her as if she should do the same. She did as instructed and removed her shoes and stockings, and washed her hands and feet in the chilly water. And it was as Mr. Thorn had said, the water sluiced off all the grime without scrubbing.

They left their shoes behind and joined the throng of revelers. She walked on the mossy ground, her toes curling in it, reveling in the sensation. She'd never walked barefoot out of doors apart from when she had been young enough for it to be charming. At the center of the garden, a bright bonfire glowed, its embers dancing on the wind.

To one side, musicians played instruments made of leaves and glimmered with golden light from the bonfire. Fae creatures gathered along tables, burdened by platters of glistening fruits in crystal bowls, steaming platters of bread and fish, and meats dripping with juices. Catherine turned her gaze away as to not be tempted.

A man with a crown made of a bird's nest talked animatedly to a woman with a hawk nose and a cloak of feathers. A woman with clever fox eyes wearing tawny pelts with hoods devoured a squirming mouse whole. Catherine turned away, her head swiveling this way and that trying to take it all in. Many wore empty-eyed masks pushed back on their heads, so lifelike it seemed they merely needed to pull them down to resume the forms of animals they once were.

She felt their hungry gazes as they passed them by. She was grateful for Mr. Thorn and stayed close enough to him that their shoulders brushed. In her other hand, she clutched the dagger. Given a chance, she had no doubt any one of these fae creatures wouldn't hesitate to swallow her whole.

At the far end of the clearing, a woman sat upon a throne carved from glimmering crystals and white stone. Her pale, silver hair looked as if it had been woven from webs of moonlight. Her skin was pale as cream, and her opaque gown shifted in the firelight, glittering like gems.

"That is the Queen of the Twilight Court. We must make our greetings to her. It will be to her pleasure we dance," Mr. Thorn said to her.

"Dance?" Catherine gulped. She'd feared as much. She'd never learned to dance. When other girls were having their debuts, she was falling asleep to the screams of the other patients at Elk Grove. She shook her head, dispelling the bad memories.

"Don't worry. I'm an excellent lead," Mr. Thorn said with a cheeky smile. They weaved their way to the front of the crowd, where a line of supplicants was similarly giving their greetings to the Twilight Queen.

Catherine watched her between her lashes. The Twilight Queen twirled a crystal topped staff between long fingers. She waved away the pair of tree women who came before them. Ray bowed, and Catherine followed his lead, keenly aware of her humanity.

"We thank you for your hospitality, my lady of moon and starlight," Mr. Thorn said.

Catherine's stomach twisted in fear. Despite Mr. Thorn's assurances, she couldn't help but feel as if she didn't belong here, and the Twilight Queen would see that and cast her out. What was most surprising was she didn't want to leave. This place she thought had been only in her imagination came to life in vivid color. She wanted to explore every nook and cranny, to listen to the stories of these strange and varied folk in the way she would lay in the sun as the small folk told her stories of their homeland when she was a child.

"Raethorn, you've brought a guest this evening?" Her

voice was sweet as honey, and Catherine felt encouraged to look up.

"I have. I hope she does please you," Mr. Thorn said.

"You may have your amusements here in my court as you always do." She waved them away as one would a fly buzzing around their head.

Catherine let go of the breath she'd been holding. Mr. Thorn got to his feet and extended his hand to Catherine.

"Lady Thornton?" he asked.

A space had been cleared around them. The musicians with their otherworldly instruments changed the song to a lively tune that her feet wanted to tap to despite herself. The crowd had stopped to watch them, and she had never felt more exposed in her entire life. Her chest tightened. She was never good in a group. A part of her wanted to run, and another part of her wanted to shed all her fear and give herself into the music, which even now wove its spell over her.

"Keep your eyes on me, forget the rest," Mr. Thorn said as he stepped in her view.

She swallowed past the lump in her throat and nodded. She took a few faltering steps closer to him. She expected him to put his hand on her hip and for them to move in the organized pattern of a dance she'd seen at Mama's parties when she'd been a girl. Instead, he threaded his hands with hers, and when their palms met, a jolt raced through her. Her eyes widened.

He smiled. "You will experience something few humans do. Enjoy it."

They moved together, and her feet seemed to know the steps without any guidance. Mr. Thorn had described it as a sharing of magic, but it was so much more. Bodies moved around them, hands linked, voices raised, and when she moved with Mr. Thorn, it was impossible to feel where his body ended, and hers began. The energy which flowed through them felt as if the very earth moved, as if they were wind, water, or fire. His face filled her vision as the rest became a blur of color and light. Their beating hearts synced, and their limbs tied together. The heady mix of emotions she had felt before tripled and tripled again.

The magic grew within her, at first a seed buried in the earth, before bursting into a new sprout which grew and grew and exploded with flowers and vines and the perfume of its blossoms on the wind. She twirled, laughter spilling out of her. She was dizzy, drunk on magic, music, and the burgeoning feeling that she could hold back no longer. Mr. Thorn let go of her hand, and she kept on spinning even as the magic stopped abruptly, even as silence yawned around her. She could see it in her mind's eye: the Great Tree with bright green leaves against a golden horizon, so large she would fall back to crane her neck and take it all in. She reached out to take hold of it, but as she did, she grasped onto nothing.

Catherine panted, reveling in the swirling sensation around her. The air was scented with a beautiful perfume. Catherine opened her eyes. The ground beneath her feet had bloomed with a blanket of clover, and overhead a canopy of vines was brimming with white, trumpet-shaped flowers.

Where had they all come from? Was it the magic? She looked to Mr. Thorn for confirmation, but he was standing back with the rest, eyes wide.

"How? It shouldn't be possible," he muttered as he shook his head.

"It has been centuries since the night trumpet has

bloomed in my court. What is it you've brought to my court, Raethorn?" The Twilight Queen smiled, revealing pointed teeth.

The fae surrounded them, closing in on all sides, and the magic faded. The flowers withered on the vine. They hadn't made them bloom. Catherine had.

12

Power bloomed around Ray. The taste of magic on his lips was like the sweetest nectar of midnight blooms and as heady as spring wine. The radiant warmth of the Great Tree enveloped him. He'd been there only once to make his vows to court and crown in his long gone-by youth. For a moment, he was transported back there—the kiss of a breeze on his trembling flesh, the scent of the everblooms, and the rush of pride in his chest as the Great Tree accepted his vows. Then as quick as the feeling came, it was snatched away like the door to the throne room slamming in his face on the day of his exile.

Ray gasped as he opened his eyes. Where his hand clutched Lady Thornton's, it thrummed with the pulse of the forest, as if the Great Tree were burgeoning out of her. He'd sensed power in her on their first meeting. Humans and fae had intermingled for generations. Fae blood made them stronger; they sang a little sweeter, their paintings a little more real. But this? Oh, this he had never seen in a human before.

Had he known, he would never have brought her here. No, he would have brought her directly before the council. Whoever she was, he could leverage this discovery to end his exile.

Lady Thornton's eyes flew open wide, and she took in the blooming flowers overhead. She let go of him and took a step back. Her chest was heaving, and her pale cheeks flushed. The tight coil of her hair had come undone, and it fell around her shoulders in gentle waves. Faery had helped her bloom. Had they not come here, he might never have realized. She'd been wilting in the human realm, and it wasn't until she was here that she could truly burst to life. This must be fate or the hand of the Great Tree itself, which brought them together.

The Twilight Queen clapped her hands together. Ray shook himself and scanned the crowd. They'd all turned toward her now, hunger in their gazes. Magic meant power in Faery. For generations, magic had been fading, births were becoming fewer, and in the small courts, there were rumors of fae born without any magic at all. Those who had little magic attached themselves to the powerful. But someone with raw magic and completely unaware of how to use it, they were prey before hungry wolves. The Twilight Queen licked her pink lips as she rose from her crystal throne. The starlight in her gossamer gown shifted and glittered in the moonlight. She allowed him into this court once a month, not out of the goodness of her heart but for his links to Thorn Court, the most powerful court in Western Faery. Before the king died, Ray had been head of his guard, privy to his most intimate secrets, and his father had been the King's right hand, his chief advisor. Ray might be exiled, but he still had connections at court. Or at least that's what he let her believe. Ray inserted himself between Lady Thornton and the Twilight Queen.

"What have you brought, Raethorn? I knew allowing you into my queendom would be in my favor, but I never expected this." The Twilight Queen smiled wickedly, her greedy gaze fixed on Lady Thornton. He may as well not be there at all.

"There must be some mistake; she is just a human," Ray said, playing coy. He wouldn't let the queen have her.

She threw her head back and laughed, and her subjects joined her. Then she held up her hand,, and all fell silent.

"Old blood. Rare, high fae blood. Perhaps royal?" she said in a sing-song voice as she paced around them.

Ray shifted in place, arms outstretched to keep himself in front of Lady Thornton.

"The royal line died with the high king, over a century ago; everyone knows that." Unless... but that was impossible. Any child of Bella's would have been nearly a hundred. It was too insane to even consider...

"Did it? My mistake." She smirked. "Then, there's no reason for you not to give her to me, in return for my for my generosity all these long years." Her pupils had gone very large, almost entirely black and consuming the whites of her eyes.

"My gratitude is great. But I owe this woman a life debt. I cannot give her to you," Ray replied.

The fae closed in, and their urgent whispers slithered around them. They were restless and hungry. Lady Thornton reeked of power, and like bees to a flower, they were drawn to her. He felt it too, that inexplicable draw. The old blood, the closest to the Great Tree, was the most potent. But even if by some miracle she had a strain of the old blood, it should still be diluted by her humanity. And what high fae remained couldn't have sired children among mortals. None of them had moved in centuries. Last he heard, they were practically stone, and their servants had to dust them like statues.

The fae superstitiously grasped at Lady Thornton's clothes, tearing at her sleeves and hem. Lady Thornton squeaked and pressed closer to him. Her hands balled up into the fabric of his shirt.

"Give her to me, Raethorn, and I will see your place restored in Faery." The Twilight Queen held out her long-clawed hand palm up as if he would plop Lady Thornton there.

Even if Lady Thornton hadn't saved his life, by the Great Tree, even if she didn't have this power, he'd never hand her over. The Twilight Queen was wicked and greedy, and she'd drain Lady Thornton until nothing remained but a hollow husk. He grasped Lady Thornton's hand and squeezed. She trembled but didn't pull away. Their palms connected, and he felt the pulse of power racing through her. It jolted through him and lit up every corner of his body. He hadn't felt this power in nearly a century. Now that it had awoken, she acted as a conduit for the Great Tree itself. As impossible as it seemed...

When he made his vows, the Great Tree blessed him with power to protect its children, in defense of the innocent and Faery itself. Since his exile, he had not once tried to call upon that power; he had thought himself unworthy. But if he were going to get Lady Thornton out of here safely, he had no choice. He tugged on the thread that connected him to the Great Tree through Lady Thornton. At first, he feared the Great Tree would deny him, but then it filled him nearly to overflowing, coursing through his veins and tingling down to his fingertips.

She must have felt it as well because she looked up at him wide-eyed with her lips parted slightly.

"Whatever you do, don't let go of my hand," he leaned in to whisper in Lady Thornton's ear. He couldn't guarantee without her, the connection would remain.

She nodded in understanding, her lips drawn thin, and her brows furrowed in determination.

Ray channeled the energy, manifesting a sword that glowed with green light and brandished it in front of him. The aura flickered brightly around it like a flame. The gathered fae took a step back as he brandished his weapon.

"I think Lady Thornton and I shall be going." He pointed his blade at the Twilight Queen.

She narrowed her eyes at the blade and then looked back up at him. "Kill him and bring me the girl." She snapped her fingers, and the fae descended upon him like a pack of hungry wolves.

Ray slashed at them, holding back as to merely stun rather than kill. They slumped to the ground as he pushed his way through the crowd. He forced an opening, and some fled in the face of his blade but more and more came to fill in the gaps, their hunger greater than their fear. The energy flowed from her to him like an endless spring, wild and green. He'd never been the best at growing spells; most of his magic study had been on defense and attack. But there was a magical rhyme mother had taught him as a boy. He focused the energy and spoke the ancient words, his accent atrocious, and his cadence wrong. But the magic, eager for an escape, burst from him and took shape, flying from his lips and forming vines wriggling like snakes on the wind. They flew out around them and tangled around the limbs of the fae who surrounded them and even tangled up the Twilight Queen.

It shouldn't have worked, but with the power burning on his lips and Lady Thornton gaping wide-eyed in shock, he didn't have time to question it. Pulling her behind him, he raced for the forest. Mist rose up to obscure their escape, the Twilight Queen's doing most likely. He ran forward heedless of direction, wanting only to put distance between them and the Twilight Court. He would never be able to return there, but if what he suspected were true, he wouldn't need to. But either way, the vines wouldn't hold them back for long. They needed to get out of Faery, but where was the gateway?

Lady Thornton stumbled, and her hand slipped from his. As he has suspected, once their connection was broken, the power began to fade.

He turned back to her, offering her a hand up. "Mr. Thorn," she gasped on all fours. "I can't... keep running." She heaved for each breath.

He hadn't accounted for the limitations of her humanity. Even with such power, she was mortal after all.

With no time to hesitate, he grasped her under her knees and scooped her up into his arms. She tensed and gasped as he did so. The voices echoed around them in the mist; they'd broken free already.

"Forgive me, Lady Thornton, but we need to move quicker," he said, waiting for her approval.

She crossed her arms close to her chest, making it difficult to hold onto her but then very slowly nodded, her gaze turned away from him. It would have to be enough for now. With the power he got from her, he channeled it to his feet, urging his steps. He ran with surprising speed, without exerting his own energy. Whether intentional or not, as he depleted his power Lady Thornton poured more in like an overflowing cup.

Her lashes were lowered, and she wouldn't look at him. Did she know what she was doing, or was the Great Tree moving through her? There was no time to wonder. Despite his speed, the voices were drawing closer as the fog began to thin. He saw their bobbing lights in the night. At this rate, the fae of the Twilight Court would overcome them, and all his efforts would be for naught. Judging from the number of lights, he couldn't fight them all, but if he could create a copy of himself...

He looked down at Lady Thornton in his arms. There was a slight flush on her cheeks. And if they weren't running for their own lives, he might have found it charming. To make this work, he'd have to test the true limits of her power, and if it failed, it would ricochet back within him and drain him, leaving them both weakened.

They approached a river overflowing its banks. The water churned with foam and debris carried from upriver. A dead tree swayed in the rapids. If he got across and knocked the tree loose, it would buy him enough time to attempt the copy. Ray glanced once over his shoulder and back at his pursuers. He could see their pale faces now and the glint of their arrows in notched bows.

They reached the rotting log, and Ray leaped onto it. It creaked, and he swayed in place, nearly losing his balance. An arrow whizzed past his ear. Lady Thornton yelped and wrapped her arms around his neck. Perhaps fear of falling into the churning rapids had finally outweighed her fear of touching him. He alighted to the other side as a second arrow grazed his shoulder. The shot stung but the power Lady Thornton poured into him healed it quickly.

Ray ran up the other bank and paused behind the trunk of a large oak tree.

"Lady Thornton, I am going to attempt something. It will take more magic, but it might be our only chance at escape. Do you trust me?"

She bit her lip. And there was a lengthy pause. "I do."

Ray nodded his head and concentrated the magic Lady Thornton poured into him, centering it on his core. The ancient words burned on his tongue as he focused his power. His skin tingled with it as the copy ripped away from them. They stood staring, blinking into perfect replicas of themselves. Ray was breathing heavily, but it had worked. Though it had taken almost everything from him.

Shouts rang out from down by the stream; their pursuit had breached the river.

"To the east, and don't stop running." His doppelganger nodded in understanding before sprinting out in the direction he had indicated.

"How?" Lady Thornton asked in an awed whisper.

"I can do much more than that," he said, a small hint of pride swelling up in him.

"They're going that way!" The fae shouted, and as he hoped, they took the bait.

He listened as their voices faded in the opposite direction. Now all that was left was finding the gateway. And lucky for him, he had just the right person to help.

"Tell me, Lady Thornton, how did you summon the gateway? Back at Thornwood Abbey?" he asked.

She looked at him wide-eyed. "I didn't summon anything. I found it by following the music."

She heard the song of the ancients from beyond the gateway? Just how powerful was she?

"Can you hear the song now?"

She frowned and looked away from him. Maybe he had been too hopeful. After all, she was just a human, perhaps with an unusual amount of power. But a human woman nonetheless.

"I can." She screwed her face in concentration.

"From where?" he asked.

She lifted her hand and pointed in the north-eastern direction. He took off in that direction, his eyes scanning the horizon in case they happened to run into the Twilight Court again. It didn't take long before he could see it in the distance. They were nearly home free now. But the door was already firmly closed, large spikes barring any entry. If they were to get through, he would have to trust that Lady Thornton's powers were enough to open it. He was still depleted from making the duplicate.

They were nearly upon it, a few yards remained, when he heard the shouts again. And a barrage of arrows came flying from overhead. Ray took to a run.

"We're going to make a run for it. You'll need to open the gateway," Ray said.

"I don't know how. You have to stop before we are be impaled on the spikes!" she shouted and tried to pull away from him.

"You can open it. I believe in you."

"How do you know?" She stilled against him. There was a catch to her voice, as if she were on the verge of tears.

The gateway was a few feet away now, and the thunder of fae footsteps followed him.

"Because I can feel the power in you. I believe in you, now you just need to believe in yourself."

The spikes glinted menacingly. If he were wrong, they'd both have their guts hanging from spikes before the Twilight Court ever got to them.

His feet pounded the ground beneath him. He turned her to face it straight on, or else any hesitation might mean it wouldn't work. They were inches away.

"Now, Lady Thornton!" he shouted.

She threw her arms out to brace herself seconds before the gateway rolled back, creating a space just large enough for them to glide through. They landed on the lawn on the other side. Lady Thornton slid out of his grip. A single arrow flew through the gateway after them and got caught in the door as it was slammed shut. The Twilight Court on the other side. Ray rolled onto his back and stared into the burning bright noonday sun of the human realm.

A bird chirped merrily in a nearby tree. She'd really done it. He laughed. They were there at the edge of the field. In the gardens of Thornwood Abbey. Lady Thornton stared up at the sky, clutching the fabric of her dress, eyes wide.

"Am I dead?" she whispered.

Ray threw his head back and laughed hard. "Far from it." He rolled over to face her. "You were brilliant. This sort of power I haven't seen it in..."

She stared up at him wide-eyed, dazed. Maybe now wasn't the time to talk about her powers. They were probably just as much a surprise to her as they were to him.

He leaped to his feet and offered a hand to her. "Can you stand?" he asked her.

She nodded her head slowly, and he put her onto her feet. She wobbled a bit, her hair was tangled up with leaves and sticks, and her clothes were a bit torn, but otherwise, she seemed unharmed.

"Will they be able to find us?" she asked, eyeing where the gateway had been. She turned on her bare feet.

"No, they might open a gateway onto the human realm, but there's no guarantee they'll find you or this place."

She exhaled. In the gardens of the human world, her clothes looked duller and sullen. As if she had been trudging through the forest and had muddied her clothes. Which would be a convenient excuse for any humans who might ask her where she had been. Time moved differently in Faery than in the human realm. What might have been a few hours for them could have been minutes or days here. There was no way of knowing for certain. Looking at the sky, it seemed it was late afternoon? On the same day? From the outside, nothing looked changed, but this old manor had changed little over his century here.

"We should get you back to the house. The humans might be wondering where you are," Mr. Thorn said.

"Edward! He left me at the cottage. How will I explain... the wolf? Are we safe from it?"

In all the excitement, he had nearly forgotten. Who was the wolf hunting, him or Lady Thornton? It was troubling, coupled with the death of those women and Lady Thornton's power. It could all be a coincidence, but his gut told him otherwise.

"You'll be safe. I will protect you. I still owe you a debt remember?" He bowed with a flourish.

Her eyes widened, and then a pretty blush filled her cheeks. "That isn't necessary; you got me out of Faery after all..." She still clung to the dagger he'd given her.

He smiled. She had more mettle than he had first thought.

"Lady Thornton, is that really you?" Mr. Rockwell shouted.

They turned as one to see his craggy face striding toward them, rake slung over his shoulder.

"I found her wandering in the forest," Ray said. That was vague enough to cover most questions.

Mr. Rockwell quirked a brow. If only he had some energy left to glamour. "I see now, and where have you been for the last week?"

"Week?" Lady Catherine squeaked.

Catherine looked at Ray with a slightly puzzled expression. If they didn't have an audience, he would have explained the time variance between Faery and the human realm. As it were, Mr. Rockwell was looking at them both with suspicious gazes.

"Lord Thornton has been worried sick. We should get you back inside right away," Ray said and gestured for Lady Thornton to go with Mr. Rockwell.

She blinked at him for a moment, hurt on her expression. But he dared not over-complicate things. Not yet. There would be time later for explanations. He watched her go, a shrunken figure next to Mr. Rockwell's bulk. If he were going to find this killer, he would need to stay close to Lady Thornton. She had to be the key.

13

Catherine pulled her knees into her chest as Miss Larson changed the filthy bathwater for the third time. Miss Larson had scrubbed her skin until it was red and dug the soil out from under her nails. She made inquiries: where had Catherine been, they'd searched the entire forest and couldn't find even a strand of her hair. But she kept her lips pressed tight together, fearful if she spoke, the truth would come spilling out of her like the steaming water being poured from the pitcher.

A week. But for her, it had felt like nothing but mere hours. The bathwater smelled of lavender, steam haloed her head, and her fingers had started to prune. She sunk down to her nose. It still felt like a dream. But even as the grime was scrubbed from her skin, she felt the tingle of magic linger, and hidden under her pillow was the dagger Mr. Thorn had given her. The only proof of where she'd been, and yet she couldn't share it. If she mentioned it, they would think her mad and lock her away. True or not, it didn't change anything.

And if Faery were real, then so was Miss Ashton's murder. Catherine sat up straight, and the water sloshed over the sides of the tub. But why did no one else believe it or notice when she was missing?

"Is there something wrong, my lady?" Miss Larson asked.

Mr. Thorn had said that she had the sight. Could that have something to do with it? If only she could talk to Mr. Thorn. But as soon as she'd arrived home, Mrs. Morgan had hurried her off to a bath, and there hadn't been a moment she was alone since. Though it wasn't said, Catherine got the impression that her and Lord Thorn's simultaneous disappearance had been noted. At Elk Grove, there was a woman who had attempted to run away from her husband with a lover. When her husband caught her, he sent her to Elk Grove. Edward might have thought she'd done the same. How could she possibly explain to him where she'd been?

"My lady?" Miss Larson probed again.

Catherine blinked at Miss Larson. She'd been so absorbed in her thoughts she hadn't tried to answer. She blushed.

"Forgive me, I was just thinking."

Miss Larson held up a sheet. "You're as wrinkled as my old Nan. Perhaps it's time to get out?"

Covering herself for modesty, Catherine rose out of the bathtub and let Miss Larson wrap her in the sheet. She followed Miss Larson behind her screen, where she'd left out a shift for Catherine to slip into. She slid it on, and the silky fabric glided over her skin. Arms crossed, Catherine stepped around the screen to stand before Miss Larson, who put on her dress. And once she was dressed, she sat down, and Miss Larson ran a brush through Catherine's wet hair. As she did, Catherine stared at her own reflection. She was pale, and there were bags under her eyes. At a glance, anyone who'd seen her would think she had been wandering lost in the forest for days. If she kept her mouth shut, none would be the wiser.

But even as she tried to soothe herself, she felt the desire to return rising up in her, like a craving for sweets or the comfort of her mother's embrace in those lonely days in Elk Grove. She wanted to go back to Faery to feel the power and to look upon the tree again.

"I'm glad you're safe, my lady. His lordship was just inconsolable in your absence," Miss Larson said as her nimble fingers braided Catherine's hair.

"I'm sorry to have troubled everyone," Catherine said on reflex.

Guilt stabbed at her like a knife. While she dreamed of going back, Edward had been worried sick for her. But where was he now? When she had fainted, he had been resistant to leave her side, but she hadn't seen him once she returned.

Miss Larson put her hand on Catherine's shoulder, and she raised her eyes to meet Miss Larson's gaze in the mirror. "There's no need to apologize. You didn't intentionally run away or get lost. And it's not as if you're the first person to get turned around in that forest after all."

Miss Ashton had said much the same. "Have you ever?" Catherine asked, feeling uncommonly bold.

Miss Larson froze, and her eyes darted to the door. "Once..."

Catherine turned around in her chair, eager to ask her more.

"What happened? What did you—" Catherine couldn't finish the inquiry because her chamber door opened. They both turned to see Mrs. Morgan filling the threshold, her expression grim.

"My lady, Lord Thornton awaits you with his aunt in the dining room," she said as she looked from Catherine to Miss Larson.

Her heart thumped in her chest. She felt as if she were standing on some sort of precipice. Miss Ashton had said she'd gotten lost in the forest as a child. If only she had gone to speak with her that day. But Miss Larson might know something; perhaps she'd stumbled into Faery as well. What if there were others like her, people who saw as the fae, who refused to speak out of fear of being labeled insane. If she were braver, she would have asked Mrs. Morgan for a few minutes more, just a moment to ask Miss Larson what she'd seen. But the dour expression on the housekeeper's face broached no challenge. Catherine rose from her seat and cast one last look at Miss Larson before following Mrs. Morgan out. She bowed as if she'd been scolded.

Catherine followed after Mrs. Morgan in chilly silence. It felt wrong to put on a gown and go about her life as usual. There was a killer on the loose. Was it that wolf who'd followed them into Faery? Or some other uncanny creature? The wolf had to be what Edward had mistaken for a wild dog that had been killing his farmer's stock. She should warn him —but how could she when she had tried to tell them about Miss Ashton's murder, and no one believed her? If she pressed the issue, would they call her mad and send her away as her parents had?

The footman stood beneath the sconces just outside the dining room. Flickering light cast shadows on their faces. Mr. Hobbs greeted her with a brief nod and opened the door for her to enter. At the far end of the room, Edward and Mrs.

Rosewood sat side by side, heads pressed together as they spoke in low tones. When she entered, Edward lifted his head and came rushing toward her, Mrs. Rosewood on his heels.

"Catherine, darling!" Edward exclaimed.

Mrs. Rosewood swept between them and grasped Catherine by each shoulder.

She tensed in her grip, and Mrs. Rosewood's face was momentarily stricken before she let her go, instead stepping back to look her up and down.

"We've been worried sick for you. It's good to have you returned to us unharmed." She shook her head.

"Forgive me. I didn't mean to worry anyone." Catherine wrapped her arms around her as she shifted from foot to foot.

"No, it was us who were remiss to not warn you better. That entire forest should be burned to the ground. It's nothing but a tangled mess," Edward declared.

Catherine's head shot up. "But, you can't!" What would happen to Faery if they did so and all those lovely old trees.

The pair stared at her brows raised, and Edward's mouth slack.

Edward cleared his throat. "I know you love plants, darling. I wouldn't really take such measures. But I was out of my mind with worry for you." He reached for her hand and grasped it, squeezing it.

She wanted to ask him where he had been all afternoon that he had not come to her side straight away. But it felt too presumptuous when she was the one who'd gone missing in the first place.

"Shall we?" Mrs. Rosewood gestured to the table, and they all took their seats.

Edward would not let go of her hand and clung to her even as they took their seats at the table. She wanted to pull away, but guilt held her in place. When the first course was served, he let go of her at last, and Catherine sipped at her food. Everything tasted bland after being in Faery. The colors of the wallpaper looked faded, and even the bouquet at the center of the table looked wilted and gray.

The footmen took away her barely touched soup. Something brushed against her hand, and she yanked it away. She looked up to see Edward watching her with a puzzled expression. She blushed and lowered her gaze.

"Catherine, you must be starved. You should eat more," Mrs. Rosewood said.

Catherine nodded.

Neither of them asked her what happened in the forest. Weren't they curious? The main course was served: a whole roasted goose served with potatoes and roasted carrots. Mr. Hobbs carved at the table and served her up a slice slathered in brown gravy. Just the salty scent of roasted meat made her stomach twist. Was this normal for someone who'd been to Faery? Mr. Thorn had warned her against eating any of the food, but she remembered the scent vividly, and this food smelled putrid in comparison. Catherine pushed her food around her plate to appear to be eating. A tense silence filled the room. The only sound the gentle clink of forks against china.

"Are you sure you're not unwell?" Mrs. Rosewood asked, peering into Catherine's face.

"I'm fine," Catherine replied. She stabbed into a minuscule bite of goose and pushed it past her lips. She choked it down. Should she ask them or bring up the topic since they wouldn't? What if they suspected and didn't want to talk about it? Were they trying to hide something from her?

"Did something happen out there, should I call for the doctor?" Edward half rose from his seat.

Catherine looked up at him. "What do you think would happen?" she asked cautiously. Even now, she hesitated to ask outright.

They were both watching her and shared a look. "Is there something you want to tell us?" Mrs. Rosewood asked.

She grasped her napkin and twisted it up in her lap. Edward said he loved her, and if he did, wouldn't he be willing to believe her? Catherine swallowed past a lump in her throat. She had to check, just to be certain.

"I've heard stories about the forest. About people who go missing and never come back. I think they said the fae led them astray…"

Her question was met by silence. Mrs. Rosewood studied Catherine, and her expression was impossible to read. Perhaps she shouldn't have said anything.

Edward laughed. "Did a bobbing light lead you astray? Or perhaps you joined a dance beneath moonlight with strange fae creatures?" he asked.

She looked down at the tablecloth, and her stomach sank. Of course, he would find it ludicrous. "I don't know. At times the shadows can play tricks on your eyes…"

He reached across the table and squeezed her hand. She didn't pretend this time and pulled her hand away. His dismissal stung. She had hoped he was different, that perhaps he might believe her…

"Don't be upset, darling. It was only a joke. There's lots of superstition in this village, but it's all nonsense. There's nothing to worry about. It's not as if you saw anything, did you?"

Mrs. Rosewood frowned and said nothing.

Catherine twisted her napkin so hard she feared it would rip. Even if she told him where she'd been, would he believe her? No one would expect for Mr. Thorn... She flushed to think of how close they'd been in the forest while they'd danced. She'd tried to put those memories from her mind, but if she really wanted to have her questions answered, it was to him she must go. Edward and Mrs. Rosewood could never understand.

"You shouldn't tease her like that," Mrs. Rosewood scolded. "Don't you see you're embarrassing her?"

"No. No. He's right; it's silliness." Catherine put up her hands in a placating gesture.

"Why don't we talk about something else, hmm?" Mrs. Rosewood prompted.

"You're right, Aunt. What about the ball? Now that Catherine is returned, plans can be resumed..."

Their voices floated over her as they discussed details of the ball back and forth. Catherine might as well not been there at all. If she couldn't make Edward and Mrs. Rosewood understand, then she had no choice but to seek out Mr. Thorn.

14

Three identical, crisp, white napkins sat in a line before three sets of ornate silverware with carved handles shaped like vines and flowers. Catherine kept her hands hidden under the table as she wrung them. The heat of Mrs. Morgan's glare burned at the back of her neck. Mama had loved to throw dinner parties; she would have known which setting would best match the good china. But for Catherine, they all looked the same. If she wanted to catch Mr. Thorn alone and ask him questions about the forest, she would need to make a decision and soon. But how could she choose? What if she picked wrong and inadvertently embarrassed Edward at the ball?

"Lady Thornton, have you made your decision?" Mrs. Morgan asked with a tinge of annoyance in her tone.

Catherine gnawed on her bottom lip. She lifted her hand, then curled it backward. She could ask Mrs. Morgan for her expert guidance, but she equally feared her scolding. Only one night had passed since she'd returned from the forest, but she felt as if her place remained uneasy. Any wrong move and all she had fought for would come crumbling down around her. Catherine's hand hovered over her three options. What choice was there to make? She closed her eyes and pointed.

"Very good, my lady," Mrs. Morgan huffed.

Had it really been the right choice? She really hoped so. Catherine's shoulders were tense as Mrs. Morgan cleared away the napkins and silverware. Now would be a good chance to excuse herself for a walk. She just prayed she could find Mr. Thorn, and he would be willing to answer her questions. None of the fae she'd seen as a girl stuck around for very long, other than the small garden faeries and gnomes who spoke in riddles. To think it was real this whole time, that she suffered in Elk Grove for nothing. Her chest constricted. Better to shove that thought away before it swept through her. If she were good at one thing, it was ignoring things that troubled her...

"Lady Thornton, a visitor," Mr. Hobbs said from behind her shoulder.

Catherine jumped, turning to face him. A visitor? But she hadn't even gotten a chance to go seek out Mr. Thorn yet. From the moment she woke, Mrs. Morgan had kept her occupied making decisions for the ball. She'd tasted various dishes the cook had prepared, had to choose music the band would play, and the gown she would wear.

"Who is it?" Catherine asked. And winced at the question. Was that too direct?

"Mrs. Rosewood, my lady," Mr. Hobbs said in a monotone.

"I'd be delighted to see her." Catherine rose from her chair. Any escape was welcome, and perhaps once their visit was over, Catherine might be able to slip away and go in search of Mr. Thorn at last.

Catherine followed Mr. Hobbs out of the dining room and to the morning room. When she reached the closed double doors, she paused. Why had Mrs. Rosewood come to visit? Was it out of concern for her nephew? Or perhaps to keep tabs upon a woman that might be a flight risk. Mrs. Rosewood had told her she could talk to her. But everyone had seemed so resistant to talk about it. Did she know something and wanted to warn her in the same way Miss Ashton had tried to warn her before he untimely demise? A chill ran down Catherine's spine.

Mr. Hobbs opened the doors to the morning room onto Mrs. Rosewood. She sat beneath the large bay window, which overlooked the forest, her head turned away from Catherine. As they entered, she pivoted toward Catherine with a bright smile and rose from her seat.

"Sorry to drop in unannounced; I hope it's no trouble?" Mrs. Rosewood said in greeting.

"Not at all," Catherine said and stood awkwardly in the doorway. Should she offer her refreshments or encourage her to take a seat? "Would you take tea?" Catherine asked.

"That would be lovely," Mrs. Rosewood said and settled herself back on the sofa and looked across to the empty space on the opposite side.

"I'll be back in a moment with your tea," Mr. Hobbs said. His balding bowed head retreated backward from the room, and then he closed the morning room doors after him.

Catherine shuffled over to the sofa and took a seat across from Mrs. Rosewood. She folded her hands in her lap and bit her lip, wondering what to do next. She unlaced her fingers, and dropped them to her side, shifted her legs. She crossed and uncrossed her ankles and glanced toward the door. How long before Mr. Hobbs came back with the tea? Should she talk to Mrs. Rosewood about what she had seen, would she understand?

"Is anything the matter?" Mrs. Rosewood prompted.

Catherine's gaze jerked back toward her. "Not at all." Her mouth suddenly felt very dry.

The door creaked open as Miss Larson rolled in the tea cart with a steaming pot of tea and two porcelain cups.

"Let me help." Catherine rose up and strode over to Miss Larson.

"There's no need, my lady," Miss Larson said, flapping her hands to shoo Catherine away.

Catherine's hands fell to her sides, and a flush burned her cheeks. She sheepishly returned to her seat as Miss Larson set the teacups out in front of each of them. She poured the tea for Mrs. Rosewood first.

"Sugar?" Miss Larson asked.

"Yes, two lumps. Thank you, Miss..." Mrs. Rosewood tilted her head to the side as she studied Miss Larson's face.

"Miss Larson, ma'am." Miss Larson dipped her head in a shallow bob.

She plopped a couple cubes of sugar into Mrs. Rosewood's tea and then handed it to her.

"A lovely girl. Thank you for taking care of our dear Catherine," Mrs. Rosewood said, smiling as she stirred her tea.

Miss Larson filled her cup and put a single cube of sugar for Catherine without asking. She hadn't even realized she'd memorized her preference. Miss Larson set down a slice of honey cake for each of them along with their tea before straightening up. A proud glow graced her features.

"Will there be anything else?" Miss Larson asked.

"No, that will be all. Thank you," Catherine remarked.

Miss Larson bobbed her head once more before rolling the cart out of the room. Silence fell once more. Catherine picked up her teacup just to have something to do with her hands but didn't bring it to her lips to take a drink. The warmth of the tea was comforting, spreading from her palms and upward. The same way the magic she'd experienced with Mr. Thorn had warmed her body, though this wasn't a tenth of the warmth of that strange magic. Across from her, Mrs. Rosewood took a sip of her tea.

"I thought the two of us might have a chat?" Mrs. Rosewood said as she set down her teacup and saucer with a gentle clink.

"I was worried sick when you disappeared, it reminded me so much of our dear Grace," Mrs. Rosewood continued.

"Who was Grace?" Catherine asked, her voice wobbled even as she tried to steady it.

"Did Edward not... I suppose it is a painful story..."

Her skin prickled at the words. This was it. The secret she felt they'd been holding back the night before. Mrs. Rosewood knew about the fae. Or at least she hoped she did. If she were wrong, Catherine would expose herself. If they didn't believe as her parents hadn't, then it would only be a matter of time before they sent her back to Elk Grove. Catherine clasped her hands together in her lap to hide their trembling.

"What do you mean?" She couldn't resist. She had to know more. She felt as if she were walking a fine line. One wrong move and everything could come crumbling down upon her.

"Grace was Edward's mother. She died when he was

young. He doesn't like to talk about her or the circumstances in which she... died," Mrs. Rosewood said.

Catherine stared at her wide-eyed. She had to bite her tongue to not demand answers. It may have nothing at all to do with the death of Miss Ashton, but something told her these tales had something in common. Why else would Mrs. Rosewood be here?

"I'm sorry to hear that." She paused and licked her lips. "How did she pass?"

Catherine's heart was racing in her chest, and her palms were sweaty.

Mrs. Rosewood's gaze flickered over to the closed doors. "Edward has forbidden everyone from speaking about them. You understand..."

"Them?" Catherine said through parched lips. She must be imagining things. Surely Mrs. Rosewood meant someone else...

Mrs. Rosewood leaned forward and beckoned Catherine closer. Heart in her throat, Catherine tilted forward. Her body felt wooden.

"The fae," she said in a whisper and then leaned back, her gaze darting toward the door.

The room felt as if it were spinning around her. She needed something to drink. Catherine grasped for her teacup and drank down her scalding tea in one gulp, burning the roof of her mouth in the process. Outside of that strange dreamlike place with Mr. Thorn, she'd never heard someone speak of the fae. At times she doubted whether what she had seen in Faery had been real at all. And yet here she was, all her suspicions confirmed.

"Are you alright? You look terribly pale." Mrs. Rosewood

rose up to take a seat beside Catherine on her sofa and took Catherine's slick palm in her hand.

Catherine's entire body was trembling. This might be reckless, but she had to know more. "How did it—" she choked on the words.

Mrs. Rosewood looked down. "It's rather gruesome. I'm not sure if I should say."

She didn't want to hear it, and yet she needed answers.

"Did they take her... heart?" She practically whispered the last word.

Mrs. Rosewood glanced up and met Catherine's gaze. Her dark eyes searched Catherine's face. "How do you...?"

"Miss Ashton." Those sightless blue eyes still haunted her. For Catherine, it had been mere days, but that grizzly scene, despite her attempts to pretend it wasn't real, was never far from her thoughts.

"Oh. No. I feared as much. Edward was insistent that we not talk about it. He didn't want to frighten you..."

"Then he knew?" Catherine asked.

"We went in search of the body after you told us about it. But it went missing..." Mrs. Rosewood looked troubled.

Then if he knew that meant she didn't need to hide it anymore. She could share with Edward as she had never been able to with any person alive. The very thought filled her stomach with butterflies. Would she get her happily ever after just like a heroine from a novel?

"We are fortunate you were able to escape the forest. If Raethorn had found you..."

Raethorn. Wasn't that what the Twilight Queen had called Mr. Thorn?

"You can't mean, Mr. Thorn. He helped me to leave Faery; he protected me from the queen."

Mrs. Rosewood frowned. "Don't tell me you've met him? Catherine, he's dangerous. That man killed Edward's mother!"

It felt as if she'd just been dunked into an ice bath. It was the same sort of feeling as when Dr. Armstrong would make her sit in tubs of ice. Mr. Thorn had been there when she'd found Miss Ashton's body. The ghost told her he was the killer. But she had taken him at his word. She had wanted to believe him.

"But he told me he couldn't hurt me. He gave me his dagger…"

"That is all part of his game. The fae are cruel creatures. They win your trust, and then when they've got you, heart and soul, that is when they strike."

"What should I do?"

"You must stay away from him at all costs. We're fortunate this time. Next time…"

Then next time, Catherine would be like the sightless corpse of Miss Ashton.

15

Ray stabbed his shovel into the soil. The earth cracked along the surface, giving way to the slightest pressure, and crumbled as he shoveled. The sad pile of damp dirt he turned over on the surface mocked him. Mr. Rockwell had ordered him to turn over the garden beds near the pagoda. With these sad excuses for tools, it would take him hours of back-breaking work. After using up all the magic, he'd gotten helping get Lady Thornton out of Faery, he didn't have enough to glamour Mr. Rockwell and get out of his duties as usual.

Since he'd been found at the edge of the forest with Lady Thornton, he was skating on thin ice. He'd made the mistake of having an affair with a Lady Thornton years ago, and it didn't end well. He'd had to flee, lie low in the forest for a month before changing his name and appearance, and finding work somewhere else in Thornwood. He would have risked it to avoid anything as tedious as gardening, but he couldn't risk leaving Lady Thornton unprotected. Knowing the Queen of the Twilight Court, she wouldn't give up so easily. And besides, there was still the matter of the murderer at large.

Ray gouged the earth again, and his shovel collided with a rock. The collision sent a reverberation through his arm, and he swore and tossed the shovel to the ground. If he had his power, he could have clicked his fingers, and this garden would be turned over and ready for planting. In the near-century he'd been posing as a gardener, he could count the amount of actual work he had done on one hand. Stomping footsteps reverberated through the ground, and the aggravated grumble of Mr. Rockwell soon followed. He was hidden by the hedges, and it gave him ample time to pick up the shovel and resume shoveling.

"Mr. Thorn!" Mr. Rockwell roared.

He paused in his digging and quirked a brow. He couldn't have seen his short break, but already he was yelling. Why even bother working if he would get scolded anyway? Even when he'd been a new recruit in the king's guard, he hadn't been this mistreated. The next new moon couldn't come soon enough… that is if he could find a low court who would take him in for the dance. Best not to think about that right now. Ray leaned upon his shovel as the troll-sized man barreled toward him.

"I've told you a thousand—" He came up short and skidded to a stop in front of Ray and the half-turned garden bed. Mr. Rockwell's thick brow furrowed as he surveyed his work, his eyes going from the garden bed and up to Ray and back again.

"Can I help you with something? I'm a bit busy at the moment," Ray asked, gesturing toward the garden bed.

Mr. Rockwell cleared his throat. "I was coming around to see how these beds were doing."

"Well enough, unless Lady Thornton has changed her mind about their placement?" Ray asked. It was a shot in the dark. But he'd take any chance he could get to go and speak with her. There hadn't been enough time in Faery to explain everything to her between the wolf and the Twilight Court fiasco.

"No. No, she hasn't," Mr. Rockwell said as he scratched the stubble on his chin. His bushy brows were drawn together. It must have been hurting his pebble-sized brain to comprehend Ray actually doing work. Or maybe he'd glamoured him too many times. It did have an adverse effect of addling human minds.

"I haven't seen her Ladyship around the garden in the past few days. I was hoping to ask her about her preference of flowers," Ray said. He was pressing his luck without the glamour, but it wasn't as if he had many other options.

Mr. Rockwell studied the flowerbeds. There wasn't any indication anything Ray had said had filtered through the gravel in his ears.

"I haven't seen her out for usual walks as of late," Ray said.

Mr. Rockwell's head snapped up. "Don't be getting any funny ideas. Lady Thornton is above you, and you'd be best to remember that." He jabbed a meaty finger at Ray.

Ray gently pushed his hand away. "I wouldn't dare to forget my place," he said behind gritted teeth. He never would have dared say such a thing to him in his prime. And maybe once he was rescued from this damned exile, he would come back here and teach Mr. Rockwell a lesson.

Mr. Rockwell nodded his head, apparently pleased by his answer. "I'll be back in a few hours, and these beds better be done by then."

Ray scowled after him. Any desire at pretense had evaporated out of him. He tossed the shovel to the ground once more. What was he thinking actually doing manual labor? Waiting on her to come to him as if he were some inferior creature waiting upon her beck and call. Whatever power she had, at the end of the day, she was still human.

He abandoned the flowerbed and headed for the manor house. The thought of entering that building of iron and wood made his skin crawl. It would be even worse in his weakened state, but once he explained to Lady Thornton, the two of them could escape to the Thorn Court together. If it weren't for the Twilight Queen's meddling, he would have taken her there straight away. But soon, his troubles would be over; even Father couldn't deny the significance of finding someone like Lady Thornton.

The white owl sat perched upon the roof of the pagoda as Ray came up the garden path. Her large golden eyes studied him. He often caught glimpses of her from the corner of his eye. She didn't try to hide her spying now. Had she sensed Lady Thornton's power as well? Or had word gotten back to his father already?

She said nothing as he passed by. Across the lawn, Mr. Rockwell worked, back bent in the vegetable garden. Ray kept to the path with one eye on Mr. Rockwell in case he turned in his direction. Luck was on his side for once. The pathway wound around and headed toward the kitchen right past Mr. Rockwell. Ray hid behind a shrub and waited to make sure Mr. Rockwell was distracted.

The kitchen yard was busy, and the back door open. Cook's shouts drifted out. A kitchen maid carrying a basket on her hip headed for the garden. Mr. Rockwell stood up to greet her. They spoke for a moment, and then she walked among the rows of spring vegetables. Mr. Rockwell turned his back to the door as he talked with her while she worked. Seeing his opportunity, he bolted for the kitchen door and slid inside in a blink.

Pots banged in the kitchen, and maids chatted together in the servant's dining hall as they darned socks. The weight of iron made his skin clammy and his limbs weak. The quicker he went in and out, the better. He crept down the hall past Mrs. Morgan's office, which was closed. This must be a sign from the Great Tree. The bottom step creaked as he stepped upon it, and he froze, half expecting all the humans to come running and demand to know what he was doing there. But none came running, and he eased his way up the stairs.

It had been years since he'd ventured into the main house and never before in the daylight. Sweat dripped down his forehead. The iron knob on the door taunted him. Touching it would burn. Footsteps approached, and he pressed his back against the wall. If he were caught, there would be questions he couldn't answer. He licked his lips and pricked his ears. What could he say that wouldn't arouse suspicion? He held his breath as the footsteps passed on by. He sighed and turned to face the door once more. No more waiting. He grasped the iron knob and turned. The iron seared his flesh, and he pulled it back with a hiss. The door opened a sliver, and he kicked it open the rest of the way.

Damn humans and their insistence on using iron in their homes. He grasped his wrist and looked at the throbbing red skin of his palm. He supposed it could have been worse. He peered out into the hall; there was no one about. Another stroke of luck. Now, where would Lady Thornton be? When he'd snuck in decades ago, he'd gone straight to his lover's bed. Somehow he doubted Lady Thornton spent her days lying provocatively in her shift.

The hall he had exited onto was lined with closed doors. He could try each one, but each wrong choice would be another burn and further weaken him. The fatigue already made his feet feel leaden.

"Has he taken it?" Mrs. Morgan's voice approached from down the corridor.

Ray sunk back into the shadows of the stairwell. By the Great Tree, don't let her come down the stairs, or all would be ruined.

"He has, but the tonic is losing its effects. It's a new moon tonight, and the symptoms are getting harder for him to control."

New moon? How had he lost track of time? Father's deadline. That must be why he had sent his messenger to see if he'd found the killer. He'd been so preoccupied with Lady Thornton he'd nearly forgotten. There was no time to find the killer. Bringing Lady Thornton to his father would have to be enough to appease him instead. But first, he had to find her.

"If everything goes to plan, he won't need it ever again..." Mrs. Morgan's voice faded away.

Ray waited for a few beats before stepping out of the stairwell and into the hall proper. He had no choice but to go in the opposite direction of where Mrs. Morgan and the man had gone. He hurried along the corridor, which ended on a sunlit room, which ancient's blessed, was open. Ray stepped inside and found Lady Thornton sitting beside an open window, her gaze fixed on the forest. A gentle breeze rustled through her hair, and light illuminated golden beams in her brunette locks. It was brief, but for a moment, she reminded him of someone he thought long buried in his memory.

She turned to look at him and stood abruptly. The book in her hand fell to the ground with a thump.

"What are you doing here?" she asked, her eyes wide as her gaze darted to the doorway behind him.

He couldn't risk them being found alone together, and he shut the doors behind him. She backed up, eyes darting around in the same frightened way she had when he first brought her to Faery. But he thought they'd come to an understanding. What had changed? Was this why she had avoided him for days since their return?

Ray held his hands up in a placating gesture. "Lady Thornton, I didn't mean to scare you. I've been waiting to speak with you to explain about your powers."

Her face flushed, and she shook her head. "You need to leave, or I'll... scream..."

He blinked at her a few times. "There seems to be some misunderstanding—"

"I know what you did!" she said, her gaze fiery, and the resemblance was nearly uncanny. But it couldn't be possible...

She couldn't mean the king's death. No one knew the truth of that day but him and Bella. Like a fool, he had trusted his king's mortal lover when she asked him to escape Faery. She'd cried to him, telling him that she missed her family, that she hated the king's glittering palace. And so he had aided her escape, only to return and learn that the king had been killed in his absence. He'd searched for Bella after that but never found her, and he had taken the blame for the king's death. Not fully, they couldn't pin him with regicide. But he couldn't remain either. His inattention had killed the king. And so, he had been exiled.

How could this mortal woman possibly know about that? Unless it had happened again and he'd fallen for those doe eyes and her innocent smile. What if her power, these murders were no mere coincidence? Her uncanny resemblance to Bella... She had been pregnant with the king's child. This woman must be Bella's descendant... He had taken her into the forest and exposed her power. Was that her plan all along? Had her grandchild inherited the blood of the ancients?

"I think it's you who hasn't been honest with me." He stalked closer to her.

She backed up into a wall, and he slammed his hand above her head. To think he'd played right into her innocent act. "Finding the gateway wasn't an accident, was it? You were searching for it. And the wolf, is he your puppet as well?" What a fool he'd been. It was all so obvious now.

The ghost, the murder, they all pointed back to her.

She trembled like a leaf, and she screwed her eyes shut, her shoulders slumped forward as if she would collapse in on herself. "I promise I will be good. Please. I don't want to go into the room." She sobbed.

The room? If she were play-acting, she was the most skilled actress he'd ever seen. Before he could question her, however, the doors at the back of the room flew open.

The hairs on the back of his head prickled. Magic. He turned to see Mrs. Morgan standing in the doorway, a faint aura hovering around her. If it weren't for the iron weakening him, he might have tried to fight her. But given the circumstances, he had only one choice. He ran for the window and leaped out of it. His legs gave out beneath him as he landed on the lawn below, and he made a less than graceful roll. Magic sizzled on the air after him, but he didn't waste time checking over his shoulder. He headed straight for the forest. It would hide him at least until he could make a new plan.

16

Catherine paced the length of her chamber, her gaze periodically darting toward the window. The forest called to her without words, as if she had been tethered by an invisible thread to it. What spell had Mr. Thorn put upon her to make her this way? Any doubts she had about his intentions were burned away now. If Mrs. Morgan hadn't come in when she did... it was better not to think of it. If it were safe to, she would have gone out into the garden to clear her head, but he might be there waiting to pounce. She couldn't risk it.

As if to make matters worse, the manor buzzed with preparations for the ball tonight. Under normal circumstances, crowds made her nervous, but this wasn't just any crowd; this was the entirety of the village of Thornwood. Tonight she would be presented to all the neighbors as the new Lady Thornton. She couldn't be worried about murders and magic fae forests. Catherine wrung her hands. She could do this. She'd come this far; what was one ball? Her first ever.

What if she tripped over her feet at the opening? What if Mr. Thorn snuck in and tried to kidnap her?

Her chest constricted. She walked over to her window and threw it open, and gulped in the twilight air. The sun sank beyond the tree line, turning the sky an ominous blood red. She closed the window again. It was better to breathe the stifling air. She resumed her pacing. Where was Miss Larson? The sun was setting, and she hadn't even come to help her dress for the ball yet.

She could dress herself well enough, but Miss Larson had her dress for this evening. The pull cord hung on the nearby wall. She could summon her, but what if she were already on her way? She didn't want to seem demanding. Catherine picked at her nails and tore one down to the bed. A bead of blood welled up, and she put the digit in her mouth, sucking on it to stop the bleeding. By the time she got her evening gloves on, she would stain them with blood. Catherine headed over to the basin of water on her dressing table and dipped her hand in it, watching as the blood dissipated in the water.

What was she going to do? When she was insane, at least she could pretend that she didn't see anything. But now that she knew the truth, she felt as if eyes were always on her, and at any moment, Mr. Thorn would jump out of the shadows and take her heart. She shook her hands dry, and she resumed her pacing. Without intending to, her footsteps led her back to the window, and she stared out at the silhouette of the dark forest against the dying light of day. It would be easier if she could fear the woods as well. But for the first time in her life, she had felt alive, as if she'd spent her entire life sleeping up until now. And returning to the dream only left her wanting. Catherine pressed her hand against the cold glass. What if Mrs. Rosewood was wrong? How could such a magical place really be that bad?

A knock at the door proceeded its opening, and Catherine spun in place as Mrs. Rosewood came into the room. She clutched her hand to her chest.

"I'm sorry. Did I frighten you?" Mrs. Rosewood said as she swept into the room with Catherine's dress slung over her arm.

"No. I was just startled, that's all. I've been waiting on Miss Larson," Catherine said with a blush. What would Mrs. Rosewood think of her thoughts? A part of her wanted to ask her if it were possible that Mr. Thorn had put some spell over her that made her long for Faery but even knowing Mrs. Rosewood would believe, she hesitated. What if that were a silly question, or what if she questioned Catherine about why she wanted to go back? She couldn't risk it.

"I saw her on her way. She gave me your dress for tonight. I guess she got a letter from home. Her aunt is terribly sick, and she had to leave straight away."

"Oh. I suppose I will need to dress myself then," Catherine said and glanced at her reflection. Her hair fell in soft waves around her face after a bath. Could she really style her hair, though? She'd only ever braided it while she was Elk Grove, and that didn't feel sophisticated enough for a ball.

"Nonsense." Mrs. Rosewood flapped her hands. "I'm happy to help. It's your first ball, after all. Here take this, and once you're dressed, I'll help with your hair." Mrs. Rosewood handed her the blushing pink gown.

The satin glided across her skin as she pulled it on over her shift. She'd never worn something so bright before. She ran a hand over it, hardly recognizing herself. Lady Thornton felt like a stranger to her, a woman who attended balls and walked with poise and grace. All she wanted was to explore the forest, bury her hands in her garden. She wasn't sure she could do this. Was she really worthy of her title, of Edward? She wanted to love him; she wanted the life of a novel. But even now, she still feared her husband's touch, and for the past few days, her thoughts had been consumed by thoughts of Mr. Thorn. Edward deserved better than someone like her, who was easily swayed by his lies. What alternative did she have? She and Edward were married now. There shouldn't be a question in her mind...

"Catherine?" Mrs. Rosewood inquired from the other side of the screen.

"Coming." Catherine stepped out from behind the screen.

"You're a vision." Mrs. Rosewood beamed, and her smile lit up her heart-shaped face.

"Thank you for helping me," she said. It seemed improper to have Mrs. Rosewood dress her for the ball, surely one of the servants could have been summoned. But Mrs. Rosewood seemed to eschew the typical societal roles. It's one of the reasons she liked her. She felt more comfortable with her than her own husband.

"There's no need for thanks. I always dreamed of having a daughter I could dress up." She put her hands on Catherine's shoulders. "Shall we do your hair?" she asked.

Catherine nodded, and she guided her to her seat. Very gently, Mrs. Rosewood ran the brush through her hair, tying it up into a bun atop her head. A few strands were left loose to hang and frame her face. Mrs. Rosewood took the curling iron from the fireplace and wound the sections around it. A faint burning smell filled the air, and when she pulled it loose, a bouncing ringlet brushed against her face. She did the same to the rest of the sections. When she finished her hair, she applied powder and the faintest hint of blush and color to her cheeks and lips. When Catherine looked into the mirror, a stranger looked back.

Tears welled up in her eyes. Was this what she could have been, had she never gone to Elk Grove? Most girls would have had their hair styled before; they would have danced at many of a ball before marrying. When she thought she was insane, she could bear all she had missed out on, but in an instant, it had come crashing down upon her.

Mrs. Rosewood knelt down beside her, taking her hands in hers. "What ever is the matter?"

CATHERINE TURNED AWAY, DASHING AWAY TEARS. "IT'S silly."

"No, please tell me."

"I don't know where I belong. I'm terrified of the ball, but I am equally afraid of what happens if tonight doesn't go well."

Mrs. Rosewood squeezed her hands. "Tonight will go perfectly. Think of this as the beginning of the rest of your life. What happened in the past is behind you."

Catherine met her gaze. It felt greedy to hope for such a thing. But if this were her happy ending, shouldn't they defeat the villain? Shouldn't she be madly in love with her husband? None of that was true. And yet there was an assuredness in Mrs. Rosewood's gaze; she wanted to believe her, and more than anything, she wanted it to be true.

Mrs. Rosewood escorted Catherine downstairs. Guests had started to arrive, and their voices floated up the double staircase in the foyer. Her stomach did somersaults. Edward greeted them at the top of the stairs. She'd been avoiding him since she returned from the forest. Mrs. Rosewood said he didn't like to talk about the fae. And she wanted to respect his wishes, but it felt as if since then, a rift grew between them. As if they were each standing on the opposite banks of a raging river.

"You look lovely, darling. Aunt." He bobbed his head toward them. He was dashing in his tails and cummerbund.

She lowered her head. She still couldn't look him in the eye. "Thank you," she muttered.

"I'll see you both at the ball," Mrs. Rosewood said and headed down the stairs ahead of them.

Catherine watched her go, wishing she had stayed. She felt more confident with Mrs. Rosewood beside her. With her gone, the doubt began to creep in once more.

"Shall we?" Edward asked as he offered Catherine his bent arm.

She inhaled deeply and threaded her arm through his. She felt strung taut, her shoulders bunched, and her nerves prickling. She'd escaped faery amidst flying arrows and flying headfirst into massive thorns, and yet walking into the ballroom, sweat slicked her palms and made her insides turn to water. She could do this. She had to do this.

The doors to the ballroom were closed. Music and overlapping voices and laughter came through. Her heart was in her throat. Edward nodded to the footman, and he opened the door. Light flooded out into the foyer, and Catherine blinked into it, momentarily blinded.

The glittering crowd parted for them, creating a walkway

onto the dance floor. She felt every eye on her as they strode forward. She put all her concentration into putting one foot before the other. She peeked once up at the crowd and, for the briefest moment, thought she saw Mr. Thorn staring out at her. She did a double take and discovered only a stranger's puzzled face. He wouldn't come here; he wouldn't dare hurt her in front of all these people.

She and Edward stepped out onto the dance floor. At one end, a band in coats and tails waited with bows poised. Edward nodded in their direction, and the first notes of their song quivered in the air. Compared to the music of faery, the notes were flat and dissonant. The guests gathered around the fringes of the dance floor, and their faces all began to blur together. Among them, she thought she saw Mr. Thorn again, but when she blinked, he was gone. She shook her head. Her eyes were playing tricks on her.

Edward bowed to Catherine. "My lady, may I have this dance?"

Catherine swallowed past the lump in her throat and curtsied in reply. Edward put his hand on her lower back, and she flinched. She glanced at the guests. Had they seen it? She tried to smooth it over with a smile at Edward. There was a faint frown on his face, but soon the music was washing over them, and he was leading her around the room. She'd never learned to waltz properly, and with each stumbled footstep, she felt their scrutinizing gazes. She swore she heard the buzz of their gossip.

Any missteps she made were blessedly recovered thanks to Edward's quick thinking and graceful movements. He led her around the dance floor, and halfway through the dance, the guests began to join them. Catherine's footsteps floundered, and her skirts brushed against the lady dancing next to her. Then, when she had to trade partners, she nearly collided with the woman whose partner she'd gotten mixed up with. When she had danced in the forest with Mr. Thorn, it had all felt so effortless, as if she were walking on air. She shook herself. She couldn't think about him or that place. Not again tonight. This was where she belonged, among her husband and the village. Faery had enchanted her, but perhaps with time, those memories would fade.

The last notes of the song wrung out, and everyone stopped to clap.

Color rose in Edward's cheeks as he beamed at her as he asked, "Shall we dance again?"

Catherine shook her head. "No, I think I need a moment's rest."

"I'll get you some refreshment then," Edward said and disappeared into the crowd.

Catherine found a chair and sat upon it. Dancers moved about the ball, their whirling figures poised and practiced. Had she not been sent away to Elk Grove, maybe she would have been half as elegant as them? She would have debuted like other girls at a young age and wouldn't shirk from her own husband's touch.

"She's got him wrapped around her finger, doesn't she?" Lydia's voice floated toward her.

Catherine tried not to look in her direction. But Lydia and another woman she didn't recognize were talking with their backs to her.

"I never thought Lord Thornton would be so taken in," the woman replied.

Edward returned with a glass of champagne. Catherine took it from him and gulped it down at once.

"She has rather bewitched him, hasn't she?" Lydia's gaze slid over in their direction.

All of a sudden, it felt as if the entire ballroom were watching her and whispering about her. They must all see her as an upstart. The bodies seemed to be surrounding her. She couldn't breathe. Couldn't think. She grasped at her throat.

"Catherine, is anything the matter?" Edward asked. He reached for her, but she backed away from his touch.

"I'm fine, just need a bit of fresh air," she mumbled and pushed past him, rushing out of the ballroom.

The double doors at the front entrance were open, and Catherine rushed out into the night. She drank in the cold night air, and the scent of apple blossoms and pine drifting on the night breeze. She could breathe a little easier.

What was she thinking? She could pretend all she wanted, but she was beneath Edward. Maybe not a madwoman but inferior just the same. Even now, Edward must be making excuses for her running out. Like Mama and Papa had always done. How long could she keep deluding herself into thinking she could be a part of society? That she belonged here.

Footsteps crunched on the gravel. She couldn't see much beyond the light cast from the foyer. Catherine took a step back as a shadow approached. Was it Mr. Thorn come to kill her? She backed up another step. She should run for the safety of the house. What had she been thinking coming out here?

"Catherine, is everything alright?" Mrs. Rosewood stepped out from the shadows.

She exhaled in relief. It was just Mrs. Rosewood.

"You scared me. I thought you were Mr. Thorn." She

tried to force a smile, but Mrs. Rosewood's expression was grim.

"Do you fear he will come for you again?" she asked.

There was a strange note to her tone, and it made the hairs on the back of Catherine's neck stand on end.

"Yes." She said it like a whisper. The wind picked up and sent a chill down her spine as it rustled the leaves of unseen trees.

"I think I can help you. Will you come with me?" Mrs. Rosewood held her hand out to her.

Despite her growing unease, she replied without meaning to. "Yes."

17

Ray paced beneath the rows of crab apple trees. The wind rustled through the leaves as an owl cried in the night. Was that his father's messenger sent to give him a warning? He looked up at the starry sky. The moon had turned her face away. Dark night, they called it. In Faery dark of the moon was a time of quiet reflection. And tonight's was the deadline. Father would expect answers. All signs pointed to Lady Thornton. After he had escaped the manor, he had been determined to go straight to Father. But as he approached the forest, he had hesitated. What if he were wrong about her?

Doubt lingered at the back of his mind. He had been wrongly accused before, and his conscience wouldn't allow him to point fingers unless he was completely certain. Either Lady Thornton had crafted the perfect deception, or she was innocent, and her life was at risk. If only he could go back to the murder site and search for clues. Or if he knew where the first girl was killed. But as many times as he had searched

Thornwood, he had not seen a single indication of ancient magic. Father's spy had been quick to destroy the evidence.

Ray stopped his pacing and frowned. Father had never been lenient before. When the king had been killed, his intervention had been only to have him exiled rather than executed. Why would his father destroy any evidence that might help him find the real killer? At first, he had simply assumed it was to cover up his murders, but if that were the case, why give him a deadline to find the killer? It didn't add up. He shook his head.

It wouldn't hurt to try and talk to Lady Thornton once more. Maybe there was something she'd seen, some new evidence she might give him. He had until sunrise before Father would come looking for answers. He looped around and headed in the direction of the manor. As he approached, he heard a multitude of excited voices, and he slowed his pace. Easing back into the shadows cast by the manor house, he watched a line of carriages pull into the circular drive. Servants from inside the manor rushed forward to greet the arrivals. The air stank of iron, and the collection of carriages and horses with their metal shoes made his stomach twist unpleasantly. The humans must be having their own dance tonight.

Normally it would have made the perfect cover to sneak into the manor. He'd slipped into more than a few dances over the years. They were stiff and the music terrible, but rather predictable. But after his disastrous encounter with Lady Thornton this afternoon, it would more than likely end with her accusing him of murder in front of all the humans. Perhaps if he hadn't exhausted all his magic trying to help her escape Faery, it wouldn't be much of a threat, but in his current state... No, it was better to resolve this one on his own.

The voices of the party-goers faded as he headed away from the manor and back to the forest. What was the point of any of it? Father wouldn't believe him anyway. Maybe instead of waiting for him to come and make the decision, he ran away at last? He could slip into a gateway, travel through Faery to faraway realms where even his father couldn't reach him. He was nearly to the forest when he caught a putrid scent on the wind. It made his stomach turn. He covered his nose with his hand. Blood magic. Had the killer struck again?

Though every instinct told him to run, he followed it to its source. It made his skin crawl the closer he got. This was stronger than the girl he'd found with Lady Thornton. It was fresh. One pale hand splattered in blood peeked out from behind a nearby ash tree. He approached cautiously, eyes flickering around the forest in case the killer was still nearby.

The young woman wore a maid's outfit. The apron was soaked through with blood. Her sternum carved open, and an empty cavity left where her heart had been. He hadn't thought too much about how the girls had been killed. Ray knelt down beside her and pulled out a rag from his back pocket to cover her sightless eyes. They'd cut out her heart. Poor girl. Ray stood. Father had been certain that the killer would strike again. Why had he been so confident?

Bloody tracks led from the body and ended at the grass where they had presumably wiped them the best they could. But the stench of blood magic would have followed them. Ray followed it across the lawn and toward the manor. Could it really have been Lady Thornton? Everything he'd learned about the forbidden magics said that they corrupted the wielder, twisting their magic and creating death and destruction. He'd felt her magic, and it had been pure as the spring at the Great Tree. If it weren't Lady Thornton, who was it?

If only he knew more about the old magics. These girls had been killed for a purpose. Three girls. Each with their heart cut out. Perhaps for a purpose? Could blood magic cure the wolf's curse? The wolf might not have been chasing him, but Lady Thornton, and hadn't he heard the servants talking about a cure? It must be Lord Thornton... Why hadn't he thought of it sooner?

Without a second thought, he dashed toward the manor house to the back kitchen entrance, but as he came around the corner, he spotted Mrs. Morgan pacing the yard. Lord Thornton must have put her there to guard. As soon as she had tried to glamour him, it should have been his first hint that something was wrong. The only other choice was the front door. Maybe he could blend in with the crowd coming in for the dance?

He dashed around to the front drive, and as he approached, he saw Lady Thornton speaking to a second woman who had her back to him. Ray pressed his back against the wall. He needed only to wait for a moment when Lady Thornton was alone, and then he could try and speak with her to warn her that her husband had been killing these women.

He couldn't hear their conversation from a distance, but the second woman turned. Bella. Ray's mouth fell open. It had been a century since he'd last seen her, and she'd hardly aged a day. Her dark hair, her heart-shaped face. It was all vivid in his mind. How she had danced in the Thorn's Court, how his king had loved her, and how she had betrayed him. She was alive.

The two women crossed the lawn and headed for the forest. Ray kept staring long after they left. He shook himself. What was she doing here? Perhaps his eyes were playing tricks on him. Unless she was the one using blood magic, to extend her life.

He had to stop them. Ray ran to give chase, but he didn't get more than a few feet when someone stepped from the shadows of the manor house. Lord Thornton had the look of his predecessors. Though Ray could not say they'd ever exchanged any words.

"I'm afraid I cannot let you interfere," Lord Thornton said.

"I'm not stopping. Your wife is in danger!" He gestured toward the direction Lady Thornton had gone.

"She is not in danger. In fact, it is you who should be worried." He stalked closer to Ray, and as he did, his body transformed, claws bursting from his fingertips and fangs pressed against his bottom lip as hair grew in thick bunches all over his body. "I think it's time we finished what I started in Faery."

※

MRS. ROSEWOOD LED CATHERINE AWAY FROM THE MANOR and toward the forest. The closer they got, the stronger the call became. She clamped her hands over her ears to try and block it out. But it was no use; the song was in her veins. It had seeped into every fiber of her bones. It took all of her self-control to not give in to the call and let it draw her into the forest and oblivion. She lowered her hands to her sides. Distant lights bobbed among the shrouded trees. It absorbed her vision; she wanted to dance until her feet gave out. To taste of the sweet wines and savory platters of delicacies she had seen at the feast. If she left the human world behind, she could have it all. No more worry, no more having to pretend.

She took a step toward the trees. The gateway was there just among the trees. The intertwined vines, with spikes that were no longer ominous but were budding with green leaves as if they were about to bloom. She reached out a hand to touch it, but before her finger could caress it, someone pulled her back.

Catherine snapped back to reality. Mrs. Rosewood's concerned expression filled her vision, and the song faded to a dull buzz.

"It's worse than I feared. Did you eat anything in Faery or drink there?" Mrs. Rosewood asked as she looked her up and down.

All Catherine could manage was a slow shake of her head. Her mouth felt very dry. The ache to return to the forest had started to fade to a dull pain. Not gone but easier to ignore.

"You cannot give in to their call. Do you understand?"

"I understand," Catherine said in a croak.

Mrs. Rosewood removed a gold pocket watch from her purse and checked the time, and then looked to the sky splattered with stars. "It's nearly time."

Catherine was beginning to find her grounding again. When she was conscious of the forest's call, she could keep it at bay, shoving it to the back of her mind in the way she would ignore the ghosts and fae she used to see.

"Time for what?" Catherine asked in a trembling voice.

Mrs. Rosewood set her satchel down on the ground gingerly and then took both Catherine's hands in hers. "When I asked you if you wanted to be freed of the fae, you said you did." She paused as if waiting for Catherine's confirmation.

"Well, I didn't tell you before, but I was taken into Faery when I was your age. But unlike you, I spent much longer than a few days bewitched. When I woke up from my nightmare, I escaped and swore I would find a way to stop them from ever hurting another girl like me. But that wasn't until I could find you, Catherine. You see, I cannot do this alone. I need your power to close the gate."

Catherine tensed. "I don't know what you're talking about." She tried to pull away from Mrs. Rosewood's gasp. What had happened in Faery, it had to be a mistake. She couldn't have made the flowers bloom... But how did Mrs. Rosewood know?

"You don't have to pretend with me, Catherine. I can feel it in you. The same power which created these portals can be used to close them for good." Mrs. Rosewood stared into her face, her expression so earnest.

Even now, knowing all she did: knowing how Mr. Thorn had killed those women, how they tricked Mrs. Rosewood into their realm, she didn't want to close it off.

Catherine pulled back. "That place, it was terrifying. But it felt right..." Catherine couldn't look Mrs. Rosewood in the eye when she said it.

Mrs. Rosewood grasped her shoulders, and Catherine gasped. "That's their spell. Once the gateway is closed, you will see what Faery is. A wicked place of death and deceit. We have only one chance, Catherine. You must help me close the gateway. If not, then more people will suffer. Is that what you want? For more women to die like Edward's mother?"

Catherine bit her bottom lip. What choice did she have?

"What should I do?" Catherine asked.

"I will do everything. You just need to stand here and help me connect with the gateway."

Catherine nodded.

She went to work. She pulled out various items from her satchel: a bundle of fragrant herbs, four white candles, a stone bowl worn smooth along the center, and three wrapped parcels. The third one was coated in a dark stain that soaked through the wrapping. The hairs on the back of Catherine's neck stood on end. Mrs. Rosewood sprinkled powder on the ground, forming a circle around Catherine and then a square to intersect that and then a triangle. Its points brushed the edge of the sigil and pointed at the gateway. At the corner of each square, she set a white candle before lighting them one by one. As they were lit, a breeze blew over Catherine and sent a chill down her spine.

She rubbed her arms and tried not to worry about what was happening. This was for the best, to protect humans from the fae. Her eyes were continually drawn to the small packages. In particular, the stained one. What could it be?

"What does this all do exactly?" Catherine asked between chattering teeth.

Mrs. Rosewood had lit the herbs on fire and was burning them in the stone bowl. Flickering smoke obscured her face, and she looked like a stranger, a haggard, old woman with sunken eyes and cheeks. Catherine blinked and the illusion dissipated like the smoke on the wind.

"This spell is as old as the creation of life. Once invoked, it will close the gateways, and the fae will be trapped in Faery forever."

Catherine swallowed past the lump in her throat. "What happens to them once the gateway closes?"

"They will slowly die. Faery cannot exist without feeding off the life in the human realm." She set the bowl of smoking herbs down between the parallel lines of the square and triangle at Catherine's feet. Then Mrs. Rosewood reached for the bundles.

"Is that really necessary? They cannot really be bad, can they?" Catherine asked, her eyes fixated on the bundle in Mrs. Rosewood's hand as she slowly unraveled it.

A stench escaped—something between a festering wound and the sharp scent of metal. It made her stomach churn. The wrappings fell away, and Mrs. Rosewood held up a mound of flesh. Catherine reeled backward, but her lowered body wouldn't obey her command. It was as if her feet had been planted in the ground.

"Thanks to the sacrifice of the few, the many will survive," Mrs. Rosewood said with reverence. She placed it on the tip of the triangle.

Bile rose up in her throat. The scent beside her was overwhelming. "What is that?" Catherine gasped.

Mrs. Rosewood placed the second bloody offering. "The hearts of maidens with true sight. Their lives had to be sacrificed to close the gateway forever."

Everything seemed to move in slow motion as Mrs. Rosewood placed the final heart at the third point. Her body prickled in the way it had in the forest, but the entire world tilted sideways. She couldn't make her mouth work. Her palms were sweaty, and her legs trembled as if they would collapse beneath her. This couldn't be real. Mrs. Rosewood was the killer. Miss Ashton, the ghost, but who was the third...

When she'd come to dress her, Mrs. Rosewood had said that Miss Larson had been called away. This must be a nightmare. She shook her head. Please. Let this be a nightmare.

"You must understand, Catherine. I take no pleasure in it. But it had to be done." Mrs. Rosewood's voice, which she had once found so soothing, had been laced with poisonous lies.

She shook her head. "No. It isn't real."

Mrs. Rosewood stepped closer, and in her hand was a silver dagger stained with blood. Miss Larson's blood. She stepped into the circle, and there was no escape. Catherine's feet wouldn't move as the dagger came toward her.

18

Ray scanned his surroundings, with one eye on the wolf who was mid-transformation. The werewolf threw his head back as he howled, the transformation rippling across his body. His small human body expanded like air being added into a bellows. His back hunched as his shirt ripped, and he screamed. Ray had heard the transformation was excruciating. Bones broke and reformed, and hair grew and covered his body. In the midst of changing werewolves were at their most vulnerable. If only he hadn't exhausted his magic in Faery, it would be easy enough to dispatch the beast.

But as it were, his options were run or try and fight with what power he had. The transformation was nearly complete. Tufts of hair protruded from his tattered clothing. His shoulders were twice as broad as they'd been before, and his arms elongated and dragged against the ground, tipped with yellow claws. Ray had to get to Lady Thornton before

Bella killed her, but the wolf was in his way. Looping back around to lose him would waste precious time. As it were, Bella might have already started whatever dark ritual she'd been using to try and take these women's hearts.

It would be the direct route or nothing at all. Ray rushed toward the werewolf. It swiped at him, but he managed to dodge the strike and pass him by. The werewolf howled in aggravation, and Ray picked up speed as he raced toward the forest where Lady Thornton's magic had started to burn against the night. Ray was struck from the side, and he spun to see the werewolf had not only caught up with him, but he had placed himself between Ray and the forest.

It couldn't have been a coincidence. Most of the infected lost themselves to an animalistic madness brought on by the changes of the waxing and waning moon. The wolf came no closer or made any attempt to attack first as if he wouldn't risk giving Ray an opportunity to slip past him again. Though he looked to be a beast on the exterior, Lord Thornton's human mind remained intact. He had suspected as much when he'd seen the tracks in the forest, but he never thought this would be what stood between him and redemption. Ray backed up a step, tried to feign to the right, but the werewolf leaped to block his path once more.

Ray paced, and the beast followed. They were near the back garden where he'd been working early today. Very casually, Ray checked for the shovel he'd tossed aside. The barest hint of the handle peaked around the shrubbery. It wasn't the blade of energy and light he had wielded in the forest, but it was better than nothing. Ray doubled back and sprinted across the lawn. The wolf gave chase, the thundering of his footsteps following behind.

Little could kill a werewolf, and at best he could do was

stun it long enough to find Lady Thornton. The shovel was where he'd last seen it, and he snatched the wooden handle off the ground as the wolf came crashing down upon him. Rancid breath and yellow teeth dripping with saliva came inches from his nose. He thrust the handle into his snapping jaws. The wood splintered under the force of the bite and threatened to crack. They tussled for a moment until the shovel snapped in half with one piece in each of Ray's hands.

With his right hand, he feigned to stab at the wolf's neck, but he ducked under that swing and left an opening for his left-handed strike to the shoulder. He jabbed the jagged end of the shovel into his flesh, and the werewolf reeled back, roaring. It clawed at the shovel embedded in his flesh. While he was preoccupied, Ray bolted for the forest.

White-hot pain burned through the back of his thighs. Ray stumbled and turned to see the werewolf draw closer, shovel still protruding from his shoulder and dripping blood from the wound. He tried to stagger away, but the wolf was quicker, pinning him to the ground with one clawed hand. He pressed him down into the grass, and his slathering jaws hovered inches from Ray's racing pulse.

CATHERINE TWISTED HER IMMOBILE BODY, BUT SHE COULD do nothing to free herself as Mrs. Rosewood crept ever closer. The dagger in her hand reflected the flickering candlelight as she raised it up. Catherine clenched her eyes shut, even in her last moments too much a coward to look death in the face. Mrs. Rosewood grasped her wrist, and Catherine thought she might retch. What a shameful end to vomit in her final moments.

The cold metal of the blade pressed against the soft flesh of her inner wrist, and she felt the sting as it parted her flesh. Hot blood seeped from her wound, and then Mrs. Rosewood let go. Only then did Catherine peek open one eye. Mrs. Rosewood picked up the bowl in which she'd burned the herbs, now nothing but white ash, and caught Catherine's blood in the bowl.

As her blood poured into the bowl, Catherine stared on in horror. Her blood and the ash mixed together, and the tingling sensation across her body turned into a faint burning as if flames had been held up against her skin.

"It will hurt for only a moment," Mrs. Rosewood said as she pressed a cloth to Catherine's wound to staunch the bleeding.

"What are you doing to me?" Catherine moaned. The edges of her vision were black; she felt as if someone had a hold of her throat and was squeezing it.

"It will all be over soon," Mrs. Rosewood said as she brushed the hair from Catherine's face.

Catherine's body shook. The darkness was creeping in, choking her; she was back in the room. The blackness—the absolute silence. No. No. She had to get out. She couldn't be locked in again. It closed in around her, she saw the faintest glow. The girl she had been curled in a ball locked in that dark room raised her head and reached for the light, grasping it in her hands. It glowed brighter and brighter until it burst from between her clasped fingers, illuminating outward, and with it, the song began to resonate through the warmth of the tree she'd seen in Faery. For a brief moment, she glimpsed it, and she felt the warmth burn through her, filling her with light.

"It's working. I can feel it," Mrs. Rosewood said

The light or the magic, she wasn't sure what to call it, she had to let it go, or it would burn her up from the inside.

"Picture the gateway. You have the power; you must destroy it, break the link between worlds for good."

Mrs. Rosewood faded away, and in her place, Catherine stood before the gateway, but it wasn't as she knew it. Before where there had been thorns, now large purple flowers bloomed, their sweet scent perfuming the air, and the door itself was twisted up with vines. If she did as Mrs. Rosewood commanded, she would never see it again, never feel this power that terrified and intoxicated again. The fae had chased her, and perhaps they were dangerous, but were they really any more wicked than Mrs. Rosewood, who had killed to stop them? She couldn't say. But who was she to seal the fate of others?

"I won't do it," Catherine said, her voice wobbling.

"You must. If you don't, think how many more innocents you'll condemn to die." Mrs. Rosewood's voice echoed around her, as if coming from far away.

The screams of many echoed in the distance. Catherine turned to find their source but found herself surrounded by fog. All that remained were her and the gateway.

"At what cost? Who is screaming?" Catherine asked, spinning in place as she searched for Mrs. Rosewood.

"You're young; in time, you will understand."

"Tell me now. How many more innocents must die?" Catherine shouted. The fog was starting to fade. The screams growing louder.

"This village means nothing. Do you think they would protect you when the fae come for you? They will look away and pretend as they've always done!" Mrs. Rosewood screeched.

The ball. The guests. She had intended to sacrifice them all to close the gateways? How could the fae's actions be worse than what Mrs. Rosewood was willing to do? All her life, she had seen them; they had been mischievous but never harmful. It was humans who were wicked. Her parents, who sent her away rather than understand, Dr. Armstrong, whose cruel treatments left her scarred, and Mrs. Rosewood, who she had thought was her ally, who in the end had betrayed her like all the rest.

Catherine turned away from the gateway as the last of the fog faded to mere wisps. At her feet was the basin holding her blood and the ash. She had regained control of her limbs once more, and she kicked the blood, letting it seep into the earth.

"You have no idea what you've done!" Mrs. Rosewood screamed as she fell to her knees and tried to save what remained in the bowl. Catherine kicked it away from her.

"I won't have any part of this," she said, chest heaving.

The dagger lay on the ground beside her satchel. They both looked at it in the same instant, but Catherine lunged first. She grasped it and turned to wield it against Mrs. Rosewood, who grabbed her by the wrist to try and stop her. Mrs. Rosewood's normally pristine hair had fallen in tangles around her face. Her face was gaunt, and she had aged by ten years.

"Listen to me, before it's too late!" Mrs. Rosewood screamed.

The power continued to thrum through her. Catherine could feel it whispering through her. If she wished, she could rend Mrs. Rosewood apart, but as terrified and angry as she was, she couldn't. She inched the dagger closer to Mrs. Rosewood until she could thrust the blade into her gut. Mrs.

Rosewood gasped and grabbed onto the hilt of the dagger. She stared at Catherine wide-eyed.

"How—" She gasped and fell to the ground.

Catherine didn't wait another moment to hear what she had to say and raced across the lawn, back toward the manor. She had to find help to warn someone, to tell Edward or someone about what Mrs. Rosewood had tried to do. As she came over the rise of a hill, she heard the snarl of a beast. Fur covered its back, and beneath it, Mr. Thorn struggled to keep its jaws from clamping down on his throat.

She'd been wrong about Mrs. Rosewood, but Mr. Thorn had helped her escape from Faery. He had shielded her from the fae that wanted to keep her there forever. She might have doubted him for a moment, but she couldn't do it again. The magic burned in her fingertips and tingled along her skin. She didn't know what it could do besides make flowers bloom, but she knew she had to do something.

"Stop right there," she shouted, throwing her hands out in front of her. A bolt of light shot from her hands and struck the creature between the shoulder blades.

It roared and reared up on hind legs and turned to face her with rows of dripping yellow teeth. Fear spiked in her veins, and without meaning to, she felt the power rush from her bursting from the ground at her feet in the form of tangled vines, with pointed spikes biting into his flesh. They grasped the wolf, wrapping around him and piercing his flesh. He gasped for breath while he was impaled in multiple places. The more he struggled, the tighter the bindings were around his body. He kept thrashing until he slowly fell limp, rivulets of blood running down the stalks of the vines.

Catherine's knees gave way, and she fell onto the ground, her knees pressed into the damp lawn. The vines slithered into the holes from which they'd burst from, and the earth closed up as if it had never been. The monster's limp body fell onto the ground in a growing pool of blood. A hand pressed to her shoulder, and she startled to look up and see Mr. Thorn, his own face splattered with blood.

"Are you hurt?"

She couldn't find words. What had just happened? She stared at the still form of the monster.

"Come on, we should get you inside," Mr. Thorn said, but it felt as if his voice were a thousand miles away.

The body of the monster had started to change—the hair receded, the body shrunk, and in a matter of minutes, a pale and bloody body lay on the ground. It groaned.

"How?" she asked, her voice a mere thread.

"Perhaps it's best if you don't—" Mr. Thorn started to say, but Catherine shook him off.

She stood on shaking feet. No. It couldn't be possible. She took a wobbling step and then another and another. Then she was running toward him. She stood over his gashed body, the wounds weeping and blood frothing on Edward's lips. Catherine covered her mouth as she looked him up and down. But he had been a monster. She had seen it.

He turned toward her, his gaze unfocused. "I should have told you about my curse. Forgive me for lying?"

She shook her head as tears rolled down her face. What had she done? What had she done! A physician, she must call for a physician. It might not be too late. She turned to run for the manor to ask for help.

But he coughed and sputtered, and then silence fell. Catherine stood very still. She refused to turn around. If she didn't turn around, then Edward would still be alive. If she didn't turn around, she wouldn't have killed her husband.

19

Ray looked from Lord Thornton's lifeless, bloodied body to Lady Thornton. Tears silently ran down her face, her back to the corpse. This was the second time she'd saved his life. The power that had burst from her—there was no denying it now. She had the blood of the ancients; she must be a descendant of the King of Thorns. She hadn't known about her husband's affliction, so her naivety wasn't an act. But why defend him, why risk her life for his? He wasn't sure what to make of this information.

"Lady Thornton?"

"Don't call me that," she whispered, her voice thick with emotion.

He glanced around. He'd never been one to offer comfort. But he couldn't just leave her here. Should he find a human to hand her off to? But that felt wrong as well. Their fates seemed to be intertwined now. In ways, he was only beginning to see. The front lawn wasn't far from where they stood, and guests were flooding out of the doors. He'd heard the screams moments before Lady Thornton arrived. Whatever Bella had planned, she was going to use the forbidden magic to kill all the guests. Lady Thornton trembled. Her wrist was covered in dried blood.

"Are you hurt?" He reached out to check her wound, but she pulled away from him.

She looked at him with large brown eyes, pain in her gaze. Perhaps it was her blood, or maybe it was something else, but if she asked him to pluck the stars from the sky in that moment, he would have done it for her. He opened his arms, inviting her into his embrace. She'd always been skittish of touch, but he didn't know what else to do.

For a moment, she eyed him, but then in a rush of apparent decision, she flung herself into his arms, small fists grasping his dirt-stained tunic. She buried her face against his chest and gasped a sob.

"I never meant—" she cried.

Very slowly, he patted her back. This is what humans did, wasn't it? She cried against him, wetting his shirt. A part of him wanted to enclose her in his embrace, but he knew better, he'd been trained to protect and serve the royal line. And he shouldn't cross any lines. But as she clung to him, his insides twisted. If only he could vanquish her guilt, the way he would any other enemy.

"Lord Thornton! Lady Thornton!" A voice shouted in the distance.

Ray tensed and looked toward the manor where a trio of figures approached with a lantern in their hand to guide their way. What would the staff say if they found him here beside Lord Thornton's corpse, his weeping widow in his arms? He'd seen the humans turn on outsiders before, and it was never good for the accused. But what to do with Lady

Thornton? It wasn't as if he could bring her to Faery. If her power were discovered...

She pulled away from him, dashing her tears with the palm of her hand. Her eyes were puffy from crying, and her face flushed.

"You have to stop her. I left her at the gateway. She wants to close off Faery from the human realm." Her voice trembled, but she was trying to put on a brave face. He rather admired her for it.

"What about you..." he trailed off. She had yet to look at her husband's dead body.

"I'll explain everything to the staff."

He wanted to challenge her to demand she let him stay by her side. But he knew how this would play out. She might have the blood of the ancients, but she was a human before all else. And their rules didn't follow that of the fae no matter how much he might wish it otherwise. If Bella were close by, he had to capture her; with two more bodies, he doubted his father would be forgiving and take him at his word that he wasn't responsible.

Ray ran for the gateway as he heard voices draw nearer. What Lady Thornton could possibly tell them to explain what had happened he could only imagine. It felt wrong to leave her alone, but he had to press forward. This might be the last chance he had to catch Bella. If he captured her, he could clear his name both for the killing of the women of Thornwood and for the death of the king.

He flew over the lawns of Thornwood Abbey, and in the distance, he felt the pulse of the gate, and on the wind, the stench of magic. He found the ritual site and skidded to a halt. The metallic tang of forbidden magic polluted the air along with the scent of blood. The hearts of the woman who'd been killed lay on the remains of a power sigil. Blood stained the grass and soaked into the earth. Ray turned in a circle, searching for Bella, but she was nowhere to be found. She'd gotten away.

Ray growled and kicked over a candle. He'd been too late again. She could have gone anywhere through a gateway to a far off realm to disappear for another hundred years. He turned in place once more and growled.

The owl landed on a nearby branch of a tree. Her golden eyes taking in the scene. "Quite the mess," she remarked.

Ray scowled at her. "And I suppose you didn't see what happened here?"

"I feel as if I should be insulted." She ruffled her feathers as she clicked her beak at him in a disapproving manner.

Why was he wasting time talking to his father's spy? He should be using this time to hunt down Bella. But as much as he wanted to capture her at last, his thoughts were once more drawn back to Lady Thornton. They would be taking the body in by now. Would they mark her as a killer, or would they see her as a grieving widow? He shouldn't have left her side... He aggressively rustled his own hair. What was he thinking? Dawn was hours away, and he didn't have any proof to give his father about the killer.

"I thought I would have until dawn, at least. Come back to me in a few hours," he snapped at the owl.

"Quite the contrary, his lordship would speak with you."

His father was summoning him, already? Had he grown impatient looking for an excuse to do away with his own son? Maybe he would be willing to show some grace. Give him more time to catch her. The ceremony had been thwarted, and no more humans had been injured. This time he knew what Bella wanted, and he wouldn't let her sway him.

"Go ahead then," Ray gestured toward the gateway.

"We won't be venturing to Faery. He's asked me to bring you to him in the forest," the owl replied.

Ray's brows rose. His father had left Faery to come and see him? Suspicious. But he kept his lips sealed and followed after her. She flew ahead and led him to the edge of the forest. A little way beyond the looming visage of Thornwood Abbey, he found his father waiting for him in the shadows of the old ash and oak that made up the forest.

"You called for me, Father?" Ray asked by way of greeting. Better to get this over with quickly.

"I didn't think you'd be able to do it," his father replied coolly

Ray blinked and looked from his father to the white owl who sat upon the branch behind him preening her feathers as if she couldn't be less interested in their conversation.

"Forgive me if I'm a bit confused. What did you think I've done?" Ray asked. His father couldn't have discovered Catherine's identity, could he? The very thought made his blood run cold. What would Father do if he had her?

"Don't play games. I grow weary of them. Tabitha told me about how you found the killer and destroyed them. To think someone with the wolf curse had lived so long among the humans."

Ray's gaze flickered toward Tabitha once more. But she had turned around on the branch, her back to him. Why had she lied to Father? He thought she was his spy.

"It was a surprise to me too," Ray said absently.

"I knew you could be trusted with such a delicate task."

Ray snapped his attention back to his father. Delicate task? His father had threatened to punish him if he didn't find the killer. What game was he playing? Now that was perhaps the most unexpected thing he thought he'd hear this evening.

"What, was this some sort of test?" Ray snapped back.

"Don't be ridiculous. I asked you to take care of something, and you did. It's as simple as that. It will look favorable upon you to the council."

Ray bit back an angry retort. It would resolve nothing to challenge his father. All that mattered was his power and place on the council. He would only have come to the human realm if it were a threat to his ambition. At first, he had assumed it had something to do with the forbidden magics. But it was more than that; he could see it now. How much did he know, did he know Bella was behind it? Did he know about Lady Thornton?

"It's not like you to come to the human realm; I should be honored," Ray replied, trying to read his father's expression.

Father wrinkled his nose and looked about him as if he were standing in a refuse heap. "I hope it will be my last time."

A tense silence followed. Ray debated if he should tell Father about Bella's plan to close the gateway. The comment might have been ill-timed. But what if it weren't? Father was ambitious, and cold, but he wouldn't try and close the gates. It would be a death sentence for both Faery and the human worlds surely...

Father cleared his throat. "Until I can convince the council to let you resume your position at court, I would have you do one more thing for me."

And there it was, the point he had been circling until now.

"And what's that?" Ray asked, trying to keep his tone light and indifferent.

"There are rumors of a girl with the power of the ancients, a connection to the Great Tree that hasn't been seen in generations of the fae. If you see anything, I would have you report to me straight away."

The message was clear. Find what I am looking for, and I will return you to court. A century of suffering, begging at low courts, and dancing to the whims of humans would be over. All he needed to do was hand over Lady Thornton to Father. The Twilight Queen had asked him the same, and at the time, he had hesitated, knowing she would use her like a puppet. Would his father be any better? He had scraped to gain power to rise to the role of regent. Knowing his father, he doubted he would want to give that power easily. Lady Thornton had saved his life twice. Could he hand her over to such an uncertain fate?

"If I see anything, you'll be the first to know," Ray said, keeping his expression blank.

Father narrowed his gaze at him and frowned. "Your cooperation is appreciated, son." He emphasized the word. As if there were any love left between them. All that kept them linked together were the frayed threads of obligation.

"If there's nothing else?" Ray prompted and turned, not waiting for a reply. He needed to get back to Lady Thornton. Now more than ever, he needed to protect her.

"Be careful, Raethorn. I would hate for you to end up on the wrong side of this," Father's words echoed after him.

He'd been wrong. This was only the beginning. And he was only seeing a few moves in a much larger game.

Ray reached the edge of the forest and waited. All the lights were on in the manor. Had Lady Thornton looked upon her husband's body yet, or had she been lost in the whirlwind of grief and chaos. If he had stayed beside her, would he have helped or hurt her cause? The humans might assume she had killed her husband, but if there were another man present, they would definitely jump to conclusions, especially after she'd disappeared for days with the same man.

Ray sighed. Humans were too predictable. It was their charm and their flaw. The wind rustled through the trees and sent a touch of chill up his spine. Ray turned. He'd been expecting company. But instead of flying out of the forest as she had done before, a petite white blond-haired woman with large, golden eyes stepped out of the shadows between trees.

"Tabitha, I presume?" Ray asked her. Father was rather predictable to send his spy. It was a risk to deny Father what he sought. He would find out one way or another. But he would do everything in his power to delay that inevitable conclusion. He owed Lady Thornton that much, at least.

"We meet face to face at last." Tabitha bobbed her head. Even in human form, there was an owlish quality to her movements. The slight quirk of her head and the large unblinking eyes.

"You lied to protect me; why?" Ray asked. Father had a certain reputation. He showed no mercy to those who stood in his way. If he would exile his own son, what would he do if he discovered his supposed spy had misled him?

She chuckled and shook her head. "You really have been away from court."

"Is that supposed to answer my question?"

Her smile only widened. "I haven't gotten my full measure of you, Raethorn. I know you didn't kill those girls.

I also know you're not telling your father about Lady Thornton, which is why he is sending me to keep an eye on her."

He bit back the questions that sprung to his mind. How much does Father know? What does he want with her? To restore the heir to the throne or to remove an obstacle to his power? Father might be ruthless, but he had always been loyal to the king. If Lady Thornton was his descendant, he wouldn't harm her, would he? Perhaps he would want to keep her a secret to maintain his regency...

"Do as you wish. You'll find out soon enough just how dull the human realm can be." Ray waved backward as he strolled away from her. Better to end this conversation before he let too much slip. She was Father's spy, after all.

"I look forward to it," she replied.

20

Catherine felt hollow. The reverend spoke, his voice a faint drone. Days and funeral preparations had passed her by in a blur. Lies she told were quickly accepted without question. And she felt as if she were standing outside herself, watching her life play out in front of her. Lydia sat in the front row of the chapel beside Catherine's immobile body, sobbing and blowing her nose as the reverend spoke. Mr. Oakheart and their two children sat beside her, their eyes cast downward. Their small frames swallowed up by the black of mourning.

Wearing black, sitting here among Edward's family, she felt like a fraud. Her soul should be cast to the deepest reaches of hell for what she had done. When Mrs. Morgan had discovered Edward's body, the lies had come easy to Catherine's lips. She felt the magic that tingled through her as their eyes glazed over, and they accepted her explanation of Edward's death. She'd blamed it on wild dogs. The same ones Edward had been trying to rid the farms of.

Their marriage had been a sham from the start. She'd

agreed to it to avoid going back to Elk Grove. But if she had known what she could do, what cruel fate Edward would meet at her hands, then perhaps it was better she was locked away. It would have been better had they never met. Had he married Miss Ashton as his sister intended. Poor Miss Ashton, for whom no one grieved because even now, no one knew she was dead. Her fault. And even knowing all the wicked deeds she had done, she couldn't bring herself to tell the truth.

She was damaged, broken beyond repair, and anyone who got close to her would be doomed to a similar fate.

The service came to a close. Catherine stood and went through the motions to lead the procession of mourners. They congregated in the graveyard, where they would put Edward's body to rest. The wound in the earth, the hole in the ground where they would lay his body. Fresh wet soil in a mound waiting to swallow him whole, to cover him as if he'd never been. Lydia's wails overshadowed the reverend's final invocations. Her children, with pale faces, clung to the hem of her skirt. A boy, perhaps four years old, and a girl of ten. It was her first time meeting them, she thought distantly.

Four men lowered his casket into the ground, and as much as she wanted to tear her eyes away from it, she refused to do so. She had to pay witness to what she had done.

"Ashes to ashes, dust to dust." The reverend grabbed a handful of dirt and then sprinkled it onto the casket.

Shovelful by shovelful, they filled in the hole. Catherine stood still—unfeeling, unblinking, praying that when she looked again, this would be a dream. She'd be back at her childhood home in her too-small bed and the sound of Mama and Papa's argument coming up the stairs. But instead, the sun beat down upon her. It should have been raining, but there was not a cloud in the bright, blue sky.

When the last of the dirt was put upon the grave, the mourners filed away. What now? Where did she go from here? She should write to Mama and Papa to tell them what happened. But she didn't have money for the post carriage to return home. She wanted to sink into the earth with him. To pay for what she did, but even in this, she was too much a coward.

"My lady?" The reverend said in a kind voice.

She nodded, and he led her to the front of the church where neighbors she'd met briefly a few nights before at the ball came by and gave their condolences. Their faces blurred together. No one mentioned the panic and fear of the ball. How Mrs. Rosewood's spell had almost killed them all. Like most things that happened in Thornwood, they were quick to forget. With time would they forget Edward too? Would he become nothing but a hazy memory?

When she was at Elk Grove, she had wanted nothing more than to forget. Thinking now, it had been selfish. For him, she would carve this deed into her heart. She would never forget, just as she would never atone for what had been done. While Edward's death was whispered about as a tragedy, no one remarked on Mrs. Rosewood's disappearance. It was as if she had never existed. Her body was never found. Perhaps she had survived after Catherine stabbed her.

A man approached her with a bowler hat in hand, and balding head bowed. Mr. Wolfe, Edward's estate manager.

"Lady Thornton, how are you faring?" Mr. Wolfe said.

. . .

No one had asked her, and she didn't know how to answer. She didn't deserve sympathy. The question threatened to undo her. As if the bindings that kept her in control would crumble. Her throat clenched, and tears pressed at the back of her eyes. She didn't deserve the luxury of tears. Like a porcelain doll who was glued back together, but the cracks were still there. And if she gave in now, she would crumble, and she wasn't sure anyone would be able to pick the pieces back up.

"I cannot say," she said honestly.

Mr. Wofle gave her a sympathetic smile full of pity. She wanted to shout, to confess to him and everyone standing in that churchyard what she'd done. But even as guilty as she felt, the fear of Elk Grove loomed larger.

"I know now isn't a good time, but when you are ready, I want you to speak with Lord Thornton's attorney, Mr. Clark."

Catherine's head was buzzing, and a headache was pressing behind her eyes. She must not have heard him correctly. "Attorney?" Catherine asked as she shook her head, trying to clear the fuzz from her skull.

"To settle the matters of your allowance..."

"Allowance?" She frowned.

"Didn't you know? Lord Thornton left his estate to you." Mr. Wolfe frowned as he looked at her.

Catherine's head spun, and she reached out a hand to steady herself. Mr. Wolfe offered her an arm to lean on. Edward left everything to her; why? She couldn't take his money. It was too cruel an irony.

"Mr. Wolfe, I must have misheard you. My son Patrick should be the heir as the next male in our family..." Lydia looked at Catherine with undisguised hostility.

Mr. Oakheart came over and put his hand on Lydia's shoulder. "Now is perhaps not the time, darling."

"No. I want to hear it from Mr. Wolfe himself." She glared at him as if she dared him to say anything different.

"There was an allowance set aside for you and the children, of course, but perhaps we should speak of this inside?" Mr. Wolfe looked at the gathered neighbors.

They were all watching and whispering. If the earth would swallow her whole in that moment, it would be her saving grace. Their stares felt like a burning brand. Catherine's shoulders rolled forward as she tried to make herself as small as possible.

"I told Edward from the start that putting her into his will was a terrible idea. And look what's happened. The ink has barely dried on the new will, and he's—" Lydia covered her mouth with her hand, and she stifled another sob.

"I didn't know," Catherine tried to plead her case. But it felt hollow. Maybe her lies hadn't been accepted as easily as she thought.

"You will say to my face you didn't know he was wealthy? That you didn't marry him for his yearly income?" Lydia said, her eyes wet with tears, and her face flushed.

Catherine's face flamed as did her neck and ears. She lowered her gaze. She couldn't look into his sister's eyes. Just as she couldn't say she loved Edward. It would be a lie. Perhaps she hadn't married him for his wealth but, she hadn't been honest with him either.

"I held my silence because I thought you were making him happy. But in the end, all you wanted was his money, and we can all see you got exactly what you wanted."

Catherine let her words fall on her like blows. She deserved as much.

"What do you have to say for yourself?" Lydia asked. She shoved Catherine in the shoulder, and she stumbled back.

She flinched but otherwise didn't move. If it would make her happy, she would let her rain down her fists upon her. Nothing Catherine could say or do would bring Edward back from the dead.

Lydia raised her hand to strike her. Catherine flinched on impulse, but the blow never came. She glanced up to see Mr. Thorn standing between them, grasping onto Lydia's wrist in the air.

"I think that's enough, don't you?" Mr. Thorn said.

Lydia stared at him, her eyes narrowed. "Who are you to intervene?" she asked.

"I'm her guardian," Mr. Thorn said. Lydia's expression blanked over. Her eyes became dull, as did Mr. Wolfe's and everyone else who was watching. The same way they had when she'd lied about how Edward died.

"Lady Thornton is deeply grieved over the death of her husband and wishes to return home to rest," Mr. Thorn said.

They all nodded in unison, and with a nod, Mr. Thorn indicated she should head for the manor. And she took her opportunity to run. Past the carriage at the churchyard gates. Over the fence that separated the churchyard from a nearby field. She'd run until her feet gave out beneath her, until she reached the ends of the earth. She couldn't take Edward's money. Hearing that he had left it to her, it felt like a cruel twist of the knife. She didn't deserve it.

"Lady Thornton!" Mr. Thorn called after her.

Hearing that name on his lips stopped her dead in her tracks, and she turned to face him.

"Don't call me by that name," she said.

She couldn't take his money, and she couldn't bear his name.

"Then what should I call you?" he asked.

"Nothing. Forget we ever met." She turned away, marching toward the forest. She couldn't go to Faery. If she returned there, she could only imagine what dangerous powers would develop. If she must, she would walk to London. Beg Mama and Papa to take her in. Maybe assume a new name or live as a beggar none of it mattered as long as she wasn't here.

"Nothing; where shall we go?" He jogged to keep up with her.

Catherine scowled at him. Was she a joke to him? "You don't need to follow me. And don't call me that."

"I didn't call you that. I called you nothing as you requested."

"This isn't funny!" she shouted. The words burned in her throat and scared birds in a nearby tree, who squawked as they took flight.

His expression was somber and partially cast in shadow. The sun was sinking on the horizon behind him. She hadn't seen him since the night of the ball. And a part of her feared looking at him face to face again. If she hadn't tried to save him, then Edward would be alive. She wanted to hate him for that, but she couldn't. And it only made her hate herself more.

"What shall I do? I don't know the name of my two-time savior," he said with a faint smirk on the corner of his lips. The wind rustled through the trees and caught strands of his long brown hair.

"I release you. Do not feel indebted to me. I don't deserve your loyalty." He stood a few feet from her. As if there were some invisible line between them that neither dared cross. She'd felt it since the forest. Just as Faery called to her, something in him cried out to her.

"Why would you say that? Do you regret saving my life?"

She shook her head. "No."

"Then let me serve you," he said and took a step toward her.

She couldn't. She took a step back.

The wind rippled through the knee-high grass as if an invisible giant brush its hands over the tops.

"You shouldn't. I'm not worth anything. I'm broken."

"That's not true."

"If you really want to help me, take this power away from me. Give me the life of a normal woman." She threw her arms out.

"I'm afraid I can't do that."

Of course, he couldn't that. It was too much to ask for, wasn't it?

"Then what can you do?" she asked, bitterness rising up in her throat.

"I can teach you how to harness your power, to learn to tame it, and its wild ways." Another step toward her, this time, she didn't step away.

The temptation was there. If she had just learned, if she just knew how to control it, maybe Edward would have lived. Then she thought of Mrs. Rosewood at the gateway, her warning against the fae. She had done awful, horrible things, but what if there were a seed of truth to her words. What if this power only caused pain?

Catherine took a step back, and then another and another. "I don't want it. I don't need any of it."

"But you do," he said. "And one day you'll see that. And when that day comes, I'll be here waiting for you."

She turned to run from him again. But in the end, there was no use. She couldn't run from Edward's last gift. She couldn't run from Mr. Thorn. And she couldn't run from her power. Now that she had passed through the gateway, her story was only just beginning...

EPILOGUE

The faint scent of incense lingered in the chapel. Orange and pink light from narrow windows flitted across the oaken pews where Isobel knelt as if in prayer. The flames on the altar flickered as the doors at the back of the chapel flew open. A chill wind blew in with it, the last touches of the winter before the spring. The wind extinguished the candles, and slender tendrils of smoke rose up from the wicks.

She kept her veiled head lowered. Her visitor strode cautiously toward her. The uncertainty plain in their cautious steps. The reverend had left her. Shrouded as she was in mourning black, he had not asked questions when she had knelt in the aisles. She did not pray, because she had long ago given up on having those prayers answered. If there were a god, then why would he look away when the fae had ripped everything from her? When they had stolen her daughter from her arms? Perhaps it was his punishment for the sins she had committed. The things she had done in search of what had been stolen from her had carved a mark into her very soul. If there was damnation waiting for her on the other side of the veil, then she would gladly pay that price and endure a thousand years of torment if it meant keeping her daughter free of the fae.

The visitor slid into the pew beside her, skirts rustling as she knelt.

"Mrs. Rosewood?" Mrs. Morgan spoke just above a whisper.

She, too, wore the mourning black. And though Isobel knew she wouldn't cry in front of others, Mrs. Rosewood's eyes were puffy, and her nose was red. They'd only just put the casket in the ground. Mrs. Morgan was surprisingly sentimental. But then again, she had practically raised Edward and Lydia after their mother Grace died. After Isobel had killed her. Strange how fate led people down twisted paths.

"You need not whisper; the priest will not interrupt us," Isobel said and stood up. She glanced once more at the cluster of candles upon the altar.

Grace.

It had been a century since she had escaped Faery. And nearly as long since they'd stolen her child from her. The descent into forbidden magics had never been her intended path. And with each ritual, she used to extend her life, the less effective it had been. She'd killed more humans than she could count. She remembered the first but not her name, and beyond that, the faces and places blurred together. But not her—she was different than the rest. The hearts of maidens were most potent, as their life potential could extend her the longest. The only thing better was the blood of the fae or their half-breed mortal children, like Grace Thornton.

Isobel stepped out from the pew and walked with a purposeful stride toward the rear of the chapel, to the double doors out onto the churchyard. Mrs. Morgan rose up to follow her, half jogging to keep up with Isobel.

"You are certain this will work? What if we're seen?" Mrs. Morgan's voice wobbled. She'd always been a doubter, even from the first moment she met her.

When she killed, they often pleaded for their lives. Their excuses were all the same. But Grace begged not on her behalf but on that of her son, Edward cursed by a wolf's bite, and her small fae abilities were keeping them in check. It had been too long since Isobel's last kill, and her hunger had been too great for mercy. But after the deed was done, curiosity got the better of her, and she went in search of the boy. Edward was a sweet, bright-eyed child with a splash of freckles on his upturned nose. She sensed the wolf curse in him. Years of blood magic had given her abilities she would have only dreamed of before. Perhaps out of guilt or maybe out of pity, she had revealed herself to his nanny, Mrs. Morgan, a hedge witch of small skill. And she taught her a remedy which could contain the curse. She promised to stay only until the next moon, to be sure it worked...

The sun was setting behind the tops of the trees, the sky a blood red fading into orange. At this time of day, her powers were at their peak. If what she attempted to do would be successful, it would have to be now. They'd delayed long enough as it was to not arouse suspicion. Around the back of the chapel was a cellar. Isobel threw open the doors. A cold wind blew from within, and though they did not keep the bodies long here, the air still had a slight stench of death in it.

Mrs. Morgan choked back a sob, and Mrs. Rosewood grasped for her hand and squeezed it.

"We've prepared for this. Do not doubt now."

Mrs. Morgan nodded her head, and they descended into the dark together. All these years, she had stayed by his side. The boy whose mother she had killed, at first out of guilt. But soon, her purposes changed to revenge. It wasn't long before she realized why fate had brought her here to Thornwood, to this wolf cursed boy. To Raethorn or Raymond Horn or Ethan Ray or Ray Thorn or the decades of aliases he used. He changed his face and his name as it suited him, but she always recognized him. She knew him at a glance though he never saw her. She had changed from the young woman in the Thorn King's court. She thought she could trust him, but he had betrayed her like all the rest. How else could they have found her? How else could they have stolen her daughter from her? She waited and watched for any sign for the day to come when he would recognize her at last, and she would discover her daughter's location. But the day never came.

Isobel assumed the role of Edward and Lydia's estranged aunt, and no one questioned the glamour. And for a time, she was happy watching Lydia and Edward grow. It filled the void left behind by her daughter's disappearance. And now, when she was so close to setting everything right, she couldn't leave Edward this way. Perhaps not her true son, but as close as one.

Edward's bloodless body lay on the table. Eyes closed as if he were merely sleeping. His face was peaceful, but the deep gashes on his skin told another tale. Mrs. Morgan stood over his body, her face stony, but her shoulders shook from hardly suppressed tears. She reached out as if to caress his cold skin and then pulled back.

"We are fortunate I was able to recover the hearts." At least these girl's deaths would not be in vain. Though they wouldn't be enough. She'd never reanimated a corpse before, and there was the chance it could all go horribly wrong. But for Grace's sake, she had to try.

She placed the hearts on his head, his stomach, and over the center of his chest. Meanwhile, Mrs. Morgan drew a circle in chalk upon the floor and set out white candles at the cardinal points. Once that was done, they each clasped hands over his body. Mrs. Morgan's hands were slick with sweat; her magic was minuscule compared to someone like Catherine. It came from a distant fae relative generations back. But what she needed was the link to the source of all magic, the Great Tree, and for that purpose alone, she would be a sufficient conduit.

They sang the incantation together, their voices humming the energy of the earth coursing through them. Not being of the blood herself, Isobel could only grasp the barest glimpse of the tree, a bright flash in the corner of her eye. The magic burned in Mrs. Morgan feared coming to Isobel, but she grasped it, wrapping it in tendrils of her own magic, hard cultivated after years. Life and death were a delicate balance, and while the tree represented life, so did she represent death. Edward's soul, which she had tethered to the earthly realm on the night of the attack, hovered next to them, staring down at his own ruined body.

Mrs. Morgan gasped as she looked at him. She tried to pull away, but Isobel dug her nails in her arm to stop her from doing so. The power reared in her like a bucking horse, but it was hers to tame, to control. She pulled, tugging into herself and then directing it through the first heart, it burned it up to nothing but ash, then the second, blackened and curled before it too was nothing but ash on the wind, and then the third. Edward's soul was drawn to his body, dragged in as the final heart began to beat wildly. His soul disappeared into his body, and the memories of the bodies' pain thrummed through her. Mrs. Morgan cried out, her head thrown back.

The first time with the forbidden magics was always the most painful. But after nearly a century, Isobel had almost become numb to it. The final heart burst apart, chunks of flesh hit their faces and over Edward's naked body.

Mrs. Morgan tore her hands away at last. Falling onto the ground in a whimpering heap. Isobel kept her legs from buckling beneath her by bracing herself on the table. The air smelt of metal and blood, and the hairs on the back of her neck stood on end. Was it enough? Had she really done it? Her skull throbbed, and her hands ached. Mrs. Morgan continued to sniffle on the ground. The seconds seemed to stretch out for an eternity.

And then Edward's finger wiggled. And then his leg twitched. Color returned to his pale skin, and the wounds across his body knit themselves back together. Then Edward opened his eyes. They darted, bewildered, around the room.

"Where am I?" he asked, trying to sit, but she pushed him to lie back down.

He would be weak for some time, and he would need to learn to hunt, to extend his life by sacrificing others. "Welcome back, Edward." She said, brushing the hair away from his face.

He blinked into the light like a newborn lamb, and perhaps he was a bit like one.

"It worked," Mrs. Morgan gasped.

"Who are you?" Edward asked, slowly looking between the two of them.

Mrs. Morgan stared wide-eyed at Isobel. This was an unexpected complication. "Why can he not remember me?" she asked.

She'd never brought someone back from the dead before, and there was no easy explanation. Not that it mattered, Edward had one job to do.

"It's better this way. We've held the funeral anyway. It's not as if he could resume his old life."

"Is that why you made me forge the documents of his will to give it all to Catherine?"

"Did I die?" he asked with a child-like innocence.

"Hush, don't worry." Isobel patted his face.

"Time is running out. You said you would do anything necessary to protect him. I need you to ensure Catherine stays here in Thornwood. I will find a way to cure him, and when we return, we will close the gateway for good."

Mrs. Morgan drew her lips into a line until they nearly disappeared. It was too late for second thoughts. She would find a way to bring back his memories, and barring that, she would help to keep him alive. No matter what, she would have her revenge, and she would get her daughter back.

Thank you for reading HEART OF THORNS book two TANGLED IN THORNS is available now. Join Nicolette Andrew's Reader Newsletter and get a free copy of the Thornwood Fae Prequel PRICKED BY THORNS.

Read on for an early sneak peak of Tangled in Thorns...

EXCERPT TANGLED IN THORNS

Catherine buried her fingers into the damp earth. It yielded easily to her touch, softened by the previous night's rain. Using her flattened hand like a shovel, she pulled back small mounds of dirt. It would have been faster with a trowel. Even if it was slower, she preferred to use her hands. There was something gratifying about the feel of dirt between her fingers. When she'd dug a hole to her satisfaction, she sat back on her heels. She raised up an arm and stretched as she leaned to the side. The sun was high in the sky and a single rivulet of sweat rolled down her spine. Winter had come and gone in the blink of an eye, and the first touches of spring were warming the garden.

A flash of red darted past the corner of her eye. Catherine froze and turned slowly. A cluster of long grass swayed in the breeze. That must be it. She turned her attention back to her precious Azaleas. Gently, she peeled back the burlap, exposing a tangle of milky white roots. She lowered the azalea into the hole and scooped handfuls of dirt onto it. The azalea didn't look like much. Right now it was nothing more than a few scrawny twigs in the earth. But in years time it would be a blooming bush filled with fragrant pink blooms. That is if the depictions in her botany books were any indication.

It had already been a year since Edward died. Because of her.

A lump lodged it's way in her throat and she started scooping dirt faster onto the base of the brush. A high pitched giggle broke the silence. Catherine's hand stilled. They were back again.

Without turning her head she surveyed around her. They never showed themselves. But they often lingered around her in the garden. At all times she could feel their gaze. She licked her lips and not for the first time, she thought of calling out to them. As a girl, small fae creatures had often visited her. They wove her flower crowns and played mischievous pranks. And she took the blame for the latter. Adult women didn't speak to unseen creatures. The villagers and staff already suspected her. She didn't need to give them another reason to think she was insane. Catherine finished smoothing the soil on top of the roots.

Catherine's palm tingled as if pricked by pins and needles. Something softly brushed against her arm. She jerked backwards. The Azalea had bloomed into the thick bush she imagined. Fragrant pink blossoms unfurled before her eyes, their petals like small fans. Not again.

Her gaze darted around the garden. How would she explain this to Mr. Rockwell, the head gardener? Palms smeared with soil, like blood on her hands. She had to destroy it. The staff of Thornwood must suspect. More than once she'd accidentally helped flowers bloom prematurely, and brought back withered plants. She couldn't control it and there was no rhyme or reason to it. She tried to hide it, tried to stay in the manor. But staying indoors was like living in a tomb. As a widow she was exiled from society for one year. And seeing as Edward left everything to her, she couldn't by law give it up. The garden was her only reprieve. But now that might even be lost to her. The other instances were minor, easy to explain away as they happened slowly. But this had been instant and uncanny. They would know she wasn't normal. And it would be all the proof Lydia and the others needed to condemn her for Edward's death. To lock her away for good.

Hands trembling, she grabbed onto a branch. It was new and limber and bent under her grip. It was beautiful and innocent. It had done nothing wrong but meet her.

She let it go. She was the monster, not the Azalea. She couldn't tear it out by the root.

"You're getting stronger I see," Mr. Thorn chuckled.

Catherine spun in place using her body the best she could to block out the bush from sight. She hadn't heard him approach. The air between them was charged. Words unspoken weighed on her chest making it difficult to breathe. A year and he remained at the fringes of her life. She should send him away, had nearly done so dozens of times but each time the words withered before they were spoken.

"I didn't mean to make it bloom," Catherine said her mouth felt suddenly dry. It felt like madness to admit it out loud, even knowing what he was.

"And that's something to be ashamed of?" Mr. Thorn quirked an eyebrow.

He brushed past her and she caught the scent of pine wafting off him. Mr. Thorn crouched down beside it. He reached for it reverently, his rolled up sleeves exposed the tanned skin of his forearms. His hand hovered over the petals for a moment before he nodded and brushed long fingers across the leaves. Mr. Thorn looked back at Catherine, she'd been so absorbed in watching him she hadn't answered his question. She lowered her gaze but couldn't hide the blush burning her cheeks.

"Mr. Rockwell or the other gardeners might have questions," Catherine muttered as an answer to his earlier question.

He stood to face her. It had been months since she'd gazed upon his face, it was as handsome as she remembered just as ethereal and inhuman as the faery realm he came from.

"There are ways to make those questions go away, I could teach you." A mischievous smile curled his lips.

There was an undeniable allure to the offer. What would happen if she could control this power? Over and over she'd replayed the moment of Edward's death. What could she have done to stop it? Had her latent powers not struck first, would Edward have tried to kill her? If she hadn't accidentally killed Edward, he certainly would have killed Mr. Thorn. If she knew how to control it she could have stopped it. But another voice whispered in her mind. These powers were the source of all her misery from the time she was a girl, it had only brought her misfortune. If she didn't see things others could not, if she hadn't killed Edward.

"I'd rather you take this power from me," she replied.

His smile fell. "You know I cannot. But your power is nothing to be feared, Lady Thornton."

This power was a curse. And this was just a reminder of why she had to keep Mr. Thorn at arm's length. She'd traded Edward's life for Mr. Thorn. She couldn't look at his face without being reminded of it. And yet she couldn't send him away either. How much longer would they be locked in this dance which only caused them misery.

"I told you not to call me that," Catherine replied. She wanted to be cruel, she wanted him to hate her as the rest of Thornwood Village did. That would make it easier to let him go, to release herself of the guilt of wanting him close by.

"You've yet to give me an alternative, what shall I call you instead? Catherine?" His eyes twinkled with mirth.

The flesh on her arm pebbled. To hear her given name spoken on his lips felt intimate and forbidden. It had been so long since she heard her name spoken aloud she'd almost forgotten the sound of it.

"I should be going." Catherine said but her feet wouldn't obey her.

He took a step closer to her, his dark eyes trained on her. "You didn't answer my question."

"Mr. Thorn—"

"Call me Ray."

She shook her head and backed away. She turned on her heel and fled from him, if she stayed a moment longer she wasn't sure what she would do. Heedless of mud puddles and rain slicked grass, she sprinted for the manor. Her booted feet slid in the grass and she caught herself in a wet earth and splattered her sleeves with murky water. She jumped up and resisted the urge to look over her shoulder and see if Mr. Thorn was watching. She was being ridiculous, and she knew it. And yet she couldn't trust herself around him.

Ready to continue the story? TANGLED IN THORNS is available now!

ALSO BY NICOLETTE ANDREWS

Thornwood Series

Fairy Ring

Pricked by Thorns

Heart of Thorns

Tangled in Thorns

Blood and Thorns

Witch of the Lake Series

Feast of the Mother

Fate of the Demon

Fall of the Reaper

World of Akatsuki

Tales of Akatsuki

Kitsune: A Little Mermaid Retelling

Yuki: A Snow White Retelling

Okami: A Little Red Riding Hood Retelling

The Dragon Saga

The Priestess and the Dragon

The Sea Stone

The Song of the Wind

The Fractured Soul

The Immortal Vow

Diviner's World

Duchess

Sorcerer (Newsletter Exclusive)

Diviner's Prophecy

Diviner's Curse

Diviner's Fate

Princess

ABOUT THE AUTHOR

Nicolette is a native San Diegan with a passion for the world of make believe. From a young age, Nicolette was telling stories whether it be writing plays for her friends to act out or making a series of children's books that her mother still likes drag out to embarrass her with in front of company. She still lives in her imagination but in reality she resides in San Diego with her husband, children and a couple cats. She loves reading, attempting arts and crafts, and cooking.

You can visit her at her website: www.fantasyauthornicoletteandrews.com or at these places:

- facebook.com/nicandfantasy
- twitter.com/nicandfantasy
- instagram.com/nicolette_andrews
- amazon.com/author/nicoletteandrews
- bookbub.com/authors/nicolette-andrews
- goodreads.com/nicolette_andrews
- pinterest.com/Nicandfantasy

Made in the USA
Columbia, SC
16 July 2022